CAROL APPLEYARD

MEOWY CHRISTMAS

BOOK 1

BAT**WINGED**

BOOKS

CAROL APPLEYARD

MEOWY CHRISTMAS

BOOK 1

Christmas
IN
Little Dickens

To All the Cats of Christmas

Contents

ONCE UPON

A TIME ON

DECEMBER 22

Chapter One

Today's edition of the Little Dickens Chronicle was clutched in the red-gloved deathgrip of Abigail Carson as she entered the cemetery of the town's church, adorned with twinkling Christmas lights and festive wreaths. It was a mild day for December in the small Oregon town, and the scent of pine needles filled the air. Cold wasn't the reason Abigail was shaking. The fact it was already afternoon and there was not a single footprint besides her own to be found in the freshly fallen snow leading to the gravestone of her late business partner did nothing to improve Abigail's Christmas spirit. It was one year to the day since Jacob Morris had been found dead in his office – now her office – which set off a chain of events which appeared to have no apparent affect on any one except for Abigail. Until today's headline that is.

Abigail uncrumpled the newspaper she was carrying – one of the "quaint" throwbacks of the mostly Victorian town that Jacob had found so endearing. She turned the headline to the gravestone, as if by some miracle it could read it.

"Look at this!" Her breath hit the December air, forming clouds, evidence to anyone who might be watching that she was talking to a dead person. "'Scroogey Surviving Partner Says Bah Humbug To Annual Hospital Gala.'" Abigail scowled at the silent gravestone and leaned further in.

"Bah Humbug!" She flipped her dark brown hair back as she straightened up again. "You really left me holding the bag, Jacob."

After a few moments of silence, she let out a sigh, sending another large cloud of breath floating away from her like a balloon. Abigail shook her head and raised her arms away from her sides, heedless of how the flapping paper emphasized her movements as she became more animated.

"I don't know why you loved this place so much. The feeling doesn't appear to be mutual. Even though I left your name on the company – Morris and Carson Developments – it's almost like you were never even here. No one talks to me about you –" She looked pointedly at the newspaper and back to the gravestone. "-unless it's to talk about the fact you held that Christmas gala every year for the hospital and I'm not upholding the tradition. Then you're missed. Any other time, it's like you didn't exist."

She wrapped her arms around herself, hugging her black wool coat for warmth, now that she'd vented.

"It wasn't easy, but I managed to keep the business together." She leaned in, again. "You're welcome." She threw her head back to let out a mirthless laugh. "And you're lucky I didn't marry that gem of a guy you set me up with. Because then there wouldn't be a business. And I'd be starring in the Real Housewives of Connecticut Holiday special right now." The thought of it made Abigail twist her lips into a sneer. "Of course, if I had gotten married and went to Connecticut, I wouldn't be dealing with this headline! There still wouldn't be a gala, and I'd be blissfully unaware of the fact." She tossed the paper on Jacob's grave.

The clock in the old church building in the cemetery chimed the hour, its chimes ringing out like a Christmas carol.

"Hnn. Time to get back to the grind. After today, there's only one more full working day before Christmas. I need to get things done before the town of Little Dickens shuts down for two weeks." Abigail stuffed her hands into the pockets of her jacket, turned on the heels of her stylish black mid-calf boots, and felt a spiteful satisfaction at the sound of the snow crunching beneath them as she walked out of the cemetery, passing by wreath-adorned gravestones which sparkled with a festive glow.

Abigail was a few blocks away from her office when she felt something cold whip past her nose. She skidded to a stop and saw the remains of a snowball splattered across the pavement, the laughter of children playing in the snow echoing in the distance. She glanced across the street towards a snowy park, where she could make out a group of children huddled behind trees and bushes. Then, an unmistakable giggle came from one of their hiding spots.

Abigail let out a stern yell that echoed across the street.

"Who threw that?!" The shock was visible on each of their faces as they scrambled out from their hiding places and started running in the opposite direction, their youthful laughter filling the air like jingle bells. Abigail called after them one last time. "Shouldn't you be in school?!" As the sound of their footfalls faded into the background, Abigail shook her head and brushed off her coat. With a shrug, she adjusted her purse over her shoulder and kept walking.

Susan Cardinal waved her phone at Abigail. Abigail glanced from her architect to the young man who had nervously stood up from his seat. Ethan, a young representative from McBane Properties, was clearly out of his element. He straightened his slightly oversized suit and swallowed hard.

"Ms. Carson, I'm Ethan Clarke. I represent McBane Properties, and I have a... proposal concerning your company." As Ethan spoke, Susan discreetly covered the model of the community center with a cloth, protecting their confidential work from the competitor's eyes.

Abigail scrutinized Ethan, a hint of amusement in her eyes. She leaned back in her chair, folding her arms. "A proposal, Mr. Clarke? Let me guess, your company wants to acquire Morris and Carson Developments?"

Ethan's eyes widened, surprised at her direct guess. He nodded, trying to maintain his composure. "Yes, Ms. Carson. We believe that in the wake of recent events, a... consolidation might be beneficial. We're prepared to make a very generous offer."

Abigail's smile was polite but cold, like a frosty winter morning. "Consolidation? How quaintly put. But let me be clear, Mr. Clarke. Morris and Carson is not on the market. Not now, not in the foreseeable future." Ethan's composure cracked under the weight of Abigail's words. His rehearsed enthusiasm ebbed away, leaving a visible unease in its wake. He opened his mouth to continue, but his words stumbled out, disjointed and unsure.

"Yes, but... I mean, surely there's..." Ethan's voice trailed off, the certainty he had carried with him into the room now a distant memory. His eyes darted around, seeking some sort of lifeline in the elegant, unyielding face of Abigail. With a final, faltering attempt, he added, "We just thought... it could be mutually beneficial..." But the words hung awkwardly in the air, unanswered. Defeated, he straightened up. "I... I see. Thank you for your time, Ms. Carson." He turned, each step towards the door a silent admission of his failed mission.

Abigail watched him leave, a small, knowing smile playing at the corner of her lips. After the door closed behind Ethan, she turned her attention back to Susan. Abigail smiled to herself; she was proud of the bright and talented woman she'd plucked out of obscurity. Hanging on to Susan was one of the reasons Morris and Carson Developments were still in business. She had given her an impressive raise not long after Jacob's death. Abigail had also given herself a raise, up to what Jacob had been making - it still irked her that even though he'd called her an equal partner, they hadn't been financially equal.

"How are the changes to the community center coming along, Susan?"

Susan, relieved that the potentially prying eyes were gone, removed the cloth from the model.

"They're all done, Ms. Carson," she said, gesturing to the drawing on top of the drafting table. Before she could reach for it however, someone opened the front door, and the sound of cheerful Christmas carols from a passing car radio filled the room.

Both women turned their attention to the door of the office as it swung open, bringing a gust of cold air that billowed Susan's papers up into the air. Susan held the papers down on the drafting table. Abigail's long fingers tightened around her pencil and her forearms pressed against the papers on her desk as her gaze rested on the person entering her building.

"Hello!" A man's voice called out from the door. "I just-" he struggled to enter the building while carrying two large white paper boxes. "Whoa!" The boxes almost tumbled out of the young man's arms as the door closed behind him. The young man stood there to collect himself and the boxes for a moment before looking up to see both women staring at him. He was wearing a long brown coat, and a long striped scarf hung loosely around his neck. His green-gloved hands clutched onto the white boxes tightly. He gave them an apologetic grin. "A Merry Christmas, Aunt Abigail!" he said as he carefully placed one of the boxes on top of her desk. He then turned to Susan and extended the remaining box towards her "A Merry Christmas to you, Ms. Cardinal."

Susan returned his smile with one of her own before she crossed the room to take the box from him.

"Thank you, Charlie," Susan gave him a bright smile in return. "I'll just take it over to my workstation."

Charlie spun back around towards Abigail. She narrowed her eyes at him and he quickly continued, "Go ahead, you don't have to wait until Christmas. Open it!"

"At least you didn't waste paper and ribbon by wrapping it." Abigail low-key glowered at her nephew before carefully peeling off the lid of the box. "That saves a lot of wasted time and effort . . ." Her voice trailed off when she saw the contents. She lifted her gaze back up to Charlie who had been hanging onto every reaction from his aunt.

"Well?" he asked, lifting himself slightly up on his toes.

"Charlie," Abigail dropped the lid back onto the box. It landed askew. "What am I going to do with a wreath?"

"Are these fresh boughs, Charlie?" Susan called from her workstation. Charlie turned to see her standing with the wreath he gave her in her hands.

"Straight from Angela's Christmas Tree farm."

Abigail occupied herself with getting the lid back on the box in order to hide the smirk on her face from Susan and Charlie. It was painfully obvious her nephew had a crush on her architect. This was entirely another excuse for him to embarrass himself. "Seriously, Charlie? And something that's going to make a mess all over?" She pushed the box toward him, the lid now properly placed.

Charlie rolled his eyes as he looked up at the ceiling, as if seeking divine assistance. "It's not like you have to water it, Aunt Abigail. You hang it on your door for a week and then you can do whatever you like with it."

"If you think it's such a fantastic idea," said Abigail with a smirk, "you keep it." She pushed the box closer to Charlie.

"I already have one, Aunt Abigail," he countered before adding in an afterthought. "Oh, I almost forgot. I'm not going on the trip up to the company cabin."

Abigail raised an eyebrow. "The trip that is AppDevPlus's Christmas present to all you programmers? Why would you pass that up?"

"You know about the trip?" asked Charlie with surprise.

"How could I not? You can't turn around in this town without one of you talking about how cool it is that you get to go up to this full amenity cabin to ski and snowboard to your little hearts' content for the holidays."

"That's fun for some people." Charlie's gaze dropped to his left foot, which he had been moving back and forth in a slow rhythm. "I was hoping to have a more quiet Christmas . . . " Charlie's foot stopped moving. He kept his head bowed but risked lifting his gaze from his foot to glance at his aunt. "Maybe with family?"

Abigail let out a derisive snort. "Sorry, Charlie. I'm not the Christmas dinner type."

"No, no. I didn't mean the whole dinner and Christmas carols thing, Aunt Abigail." He carefully considered his next words. "I just thought maybe we could go to Margot's Cocoa Cafe for a little bit on Christmas Eve, or Christmas morning."

"That doesn't sound like an unreasonable request, Ms. Carson." Susan said from the safety of her workstation.

The door to the office opened again. This time two people hovered in the doorway. Doctors Wong and Ifhram from the Little Dickens Hospital hesitated when they took in the scene they had walked in on. Ms. Carson was giving her architect Ms. Cardinal a nasty side-eye while, standing in front of them, the young Mr. Carson was covering his mouth. They weren't sure if he was open-mouthed from something astonishing they missed or if he was trying to hide a smile.

"If this is a bad time, we can come back." Dr. Ifhram said.

"Saved, the both of you, by the good doctors." Abigail pushed back her chair and stood up. Charlie waved goodbye to Susan as he slunk behind the doctors to the open door. He stuck his head back in to say, "Good luck!" and ducked out again, shutting the door behind him.

"Dr. Ifhram, Dr. Wong." Abigail indicated two chairs in front of her desk. "Please, won't you sit down?"

The doctors each sat down, thanking Abigail as they did so. Abigail pulled her chair back up behind her and sat down. She placed her hands on top of her desk, intertwining her fingers.

"Now, to what do I owe this pleasure?"

Dr. Wong cleared his throat. "Ms. Carson, as you know, for the past ten years Mr. Morris hosted a Christmas Gala with proceeds going to the Hospital."

"Indeed, I do know, Dr. Wong. I was here for each of those ten years. And as an equal partner for the past four, I was well aware of Jacob's misplaced altruism."

"Misplaced? Surely, you don't mean that Ms. Carson." Dr. Ifhram said, sitting back in surprise. "The hospital has been able to provide many benefits to the community due to the Christmas Gala."

Abigail brought her hands up to her forehead and inhaled. "So you have said. And I told you last year after Jacob was dead and buried - so was the Gala." Abigail brought her hands back down to the desk and looked from one doctor to the other. "That was Jacob's thing, not mine. I don't know how much clearer I could have made the fact that I would not be carrying on the tradition."

Both doctors had to avert their gaze from Abigail's face. Susan slid down into her chair at her workstation, not wanting to get pulled into the vortex of awkwardness that was forming over at Ms. Carson's desk.

"We hoped you would reconsider as Christmas grew near."

"That was rather foolish of you, wasn't it? Because here we are three days away from Christmas and you are sitting in my office still going on about the Gala when you could have gone out and found someone else to hold one for you."

This time both doctors recoiled in horror.

"Oh, no! No one would have ever done that!" said Dr. Wong.

"We could never have asked someone else to hold a Gala. Not the year after Ja- I mean Mr. Morris had died. That would have been disrespectful." said Dr. Ifhram, her Christmas-theme earrings jingling as she shook her head.

"No one would have touched it." Dr. Wong shook his head, his reindeer antler headband wobbling.

"We understand that it may have been too soon to have a Gala." Dr. Ifhram continued, "So we are instead presenting the businesses and companies of Little Dickens with a straight up donation opportunity for a new initiative we will be starting in the new year once the funds have been raised."

"Oh, really? And how is that working out for you?" Abigail sat back in her chair and folded her arms across her chest.

"Extremely well. We are seventy-five percent of our goal." Dr. Wong relished the opportunity to deliver this information.

"Once people heard about the program we are launching, they were more than happy to support it." Dr. Ifhram gave Dr. Wong a sharp glare of warning. They were here for a donation. Not to antagonize an already antagonistic Abigail Carson.

"And what exactly is this program?" Abigail asked, intrigued in spite of herself.

"It's called 'Feline Fine and Canine Cuddles,'" Dr. Ifhram opened up the tan brown attache she had on her lap and pulled out a flier. She held it out for Abigail to take. "It's an animal assisted therapy program specifically for the children's ward. But we hope to expand it to palliative care with further funding."

"The hospital is no place for animals." Abigail ignored the piece of paper in Dr. Ifhram's hand and pushed herself up, leaning with the palms of her hands on the desk. "Animals make people sick. " She looked from Dr. Wong to Dr. Ifhram in disbelief. "They can even kill them if someone has a severe enough allergy." Exactly why was it she was the one that had to say this, to a pair of doctors? "Perhaps your committee hasn't thought this new program through. Clearly they weren't thinking about any allergy sufferers that might be in the hospital when they came up with the idea."

"It wasn't our idea, Ms. Carson. If you take a look at this paper about the program, you'll see it was developed by-"

"Well, whoever it was that thought it up, then. Go back to the drawing board. And, speaking of which-" Abigail stood up straight and pointed to the 3D printed model beside the drafting table. "-This company already gives plenty of support to the community. This Community Center project will provide jobs for residents. The building will bring more businesses and tourism to the area. It's the gift that keeps on giving!"

Dr. Wong looked thoughtful. "Well, we can't really argue with that-"

"Good!" Abigail said.

"But what we're asking for is specific to the Hospital," said Dr. Ifrham. She had stopped holding the paper out, realizing Abigail had no intention of looking at it at the moment.

"Of course, you want more, more, more, more, more, more. And in order to be seen as a 'good person' around here, you want me to give money to a program that will shut down in a year because of budget cuts."

The doctors exchanged looks of confusion. Budget cuts? Where did that come from?

Abigail didn't bother explaining. "No, thanks." She picked up the box containing the wreath from Charlie and walked over to the door.

"I'm sure you two have many other people to talk to about this little program of yours, so I'll let you get on your way." Abigail opened the door. The doctors got up from their chairs.

"I'll just leave this for you to take a look at when you've had a chance to-. Well, when you get the chance." said Dr. Ifhram, putting the paper on Abigail's desktop.

"That sounds like a splendid idea." Abigail stepped aside to let the doctors exit. As they left, she couldn't resist one final touch. "Oh, just to show there are no hard feelings – here!" Abigail shoved the box onto the exiting doctors. "Have a wreath!" And shut the door behind them.

Abigail's fists were clenched as she stomped across the room to her desk. She snatched the paper off her desk, balled it up, and shoved it into the garbage can by her desk with more force than was necessary. She yanked open one of her desk drawers, pulled out a wipe and scrubbed at her hands.

"Well, I can see I'm not going to get any more work done if I stay here." Abigail switched the wipe to clean her other hand. "I'm going to pack up and work from my office at home, Susan." She dropped the wipe into the garbage can. "Be a dear and lock up when you leave at five."

Abigail put on her coat, wound her scarf around her neck, collected her purse before shoving her laptop into its bag. She walked out of the office, giving a slightly cheerful wave to Susan.

"Sure thing, Ms. Carson." Susan waved back. She knew any cheerfulness in the wave was not directed at her. She brought the wreath Charlie gave her close to her nose and inhaled deeply. The sharp tang of the fresh boughs helped to lift her mood. She moved to put the wreath back in the box. She hesitated. Shook her head at herself for being indecisive and put it in the box and put on the lid. She sat down at her workstation and sighed. She looked around at the empty office. A slow smile crept over her face.

Susan pulled on her coat, grabbed her keys out of her purse and headed to her hatchback parked a few doors down from the office. She popped the trunk and pulled out a medium tote bin and a green canvas roll about three feet in height. She closed the trunk and brought the items into the office.

She cleared off the small table reserved for promotional material. She took off her coat. She pulled out her phone from her purse and sent a text message:

SUSAN:Boss went home early. Closing up at 5. Any requests?

T-BIRD:Yes, you need to get a new job.

SUSAN:Lol, I meant for take out.

T-BIRD:I'm serious RB, get a new job.

SUSAN:I'm calling you.

Susan pressed the number labeled T-BIRD as she walked over to the small table, put the speakerphone on and set the phone down.

"Take out isn't a phone call," a male voice answered the phone.

"It became one once you started talking about me getting a new job." Susan unzipped the green canvas roll, pulled out the table-top artificial tree and set it on the table.

"Can you blame me? Who would blame you? She left early and you're left there to close up. You can do so much more at another company. You got another letter from that one in California."

"No, Tim," Susan's tone was sharp. "We aren't having this conversation on the phone, while I'm at work. Abigail gave me a chance when no one else, including that company, would consider an Indigenous, female architect. I'm not leaving because things have gotten a little challenging."

"I thought we weren't having this conversation on the phone, Sis." Susan heard the snicker in his voice.

"It's just-I worry about her, Tim." Susan straightened the branches of the artificial tree. "You say she left early but she's going home to do more work." Susan opened the tote bin and took out some Christmas ornaments. "Today, a guy from McBane Properties came in with some proposal to buy us out. You should've seen her handle him. Abigail was so direct, shut him down before he could even get his pitch off the ground." She chuckled, remembering the scene. "The poor guy didn't stand a chance. Left looking like a scolded schoolboy. It's more than just work for her; it's about holding on to what she and Jacob built. She left early because people were coming in and pestering her about Christmas. She was almost skipping out the door." The ornament in her hand jingled as she waved it in the direction of the door as though he could see her.

"I'm having a hard time imagining that."

"It's true. You know why? Because she knows no one would dare bother her at home. Here, she's as fair game as any other person in the town." Susan continued putting decorations on the tree. "But locked up in the house . . . She's as unreachable as if she stepped onto an airplane and flew to another country. "

"Oh, yes, please. That would be a Christmas to celebrate."

"Don't be mean. You know she's all alone in the house of her former business partner and mentor. I know losing someone can change a person. Burying herself in work hasn't helped her the way she thinks it has." She wrapped a strand of rainbow gradient garland around the small tree.

"You should tell her that. Oh, wait. You already have. Several times."

"Maybe I should invite her over and you can tell her. Since she doesn't listen to me."

"You wouldn't dare!" Panic surged through Tim's voice.

"Relax. She wouldn't accept anyway. She won't even meet her nephew in public on Christmas Eve or Christmas day, even." Susan wound a set of battery powered led lights through the branches, knocking some ornaments askew and some completely off the tree.

"And you think I'm hardcore. You put the ornaments on before the garland and lights again, didn't you?"

"Not everyone's wounds are visible, Tim. And, yes, yes I did."

"I wish mine wasn't."

"Would you really want to trade one pain for another?" Susan's brow furrowed as she corralled the scattered ornaments. She was pleased with her decorating skills. The *conversation* concerned her in more ways than one.

"Not when you put it like that."

Susan put the ornaments she had in her hands back on the tree.

"You still there?"

"Just thinking. I worry about her." *I worry about you.* Susan didn't say. She sighed and inspected her handiwork, wishing she could do more for them than worry.

Abigail navigated her way up the snow-covered road, the tires of her car crunching in the silence. The road winding up to the house hadn't been plowed yet. She was the only one on the road. Her mind, unguarded in the solitude of her car, replayed the events of the day, particularly Ethan Clarke's audacious proposal.

The nerve of McBane Properties, thinking they could simply swoop in and buy out Morris and Carson Developments. The sheer audacity of the offer irked her more now in the quiet of her car than it had in the moment. She could still picture Ethan's face, full of misguided confidence, dissolving into uncertainty as she rejected his proposal. It wasn't only the offer itself; it was what it represented – the constant underestimation and challenges she faced in an industry that still seemed to doubt her, even after all her successes.

As these thoughts churned in her mind, the snow-filled clouds above darkened the sky, the cold seeping in. The car's headlights cut through a world of swirling snowflakes, a hypnotic and isolating white canvas.

Then, suddenly, a small animal darted through the beams of her headlights. Jolted from her brooding, Abigail gripped the steering wheel and stomped on the brakes. The car fishtailed on the slippery road and skidded to a stop on the shoulder.

"Stupid!" Abigail slapped her hands on the steering wheel. It had taken her a few moments to register what just happened. "You know better than to slam on the brakes in these road conditions!" She put her elbows on the steering wheel, supporting her head with her hands. She was so disappointed in herself. The only thing that made it better was that no one had witnessed her humiliation. Okay, two things. Whatever it was that had run across the road, she hadn't hit it. That would have been worse than ending up in this road's equivalent of a ditch. *What was it? A dog? A cat? Maybe even a fox.* Abigail wasn't sure. Thinking about that helped her to calm down. Abigail was feeling good enough now to let out a sigh. She could see her breath. She squinted at the car's dashboard and saw that the car had stalled out. How long had she been sitting there? It was still snowing. She bit her lip as she turned the key. She let out another sigh of relief and smiled up at the roof as the engine turned.

A few miles later, she pulled into her driveway. She had lived here for almost a year now and it still felt surreal, like the events of the drive tonight, with the near miss she'd had on the road. She could almost hear Jacob's laughter ringing out as she pictured herself walking through the door, arms flailing with indignation about the slippery conditions. It had been a few winters since they had that conversation, although no animals were involved back then.

She got out of the car and started walking to the front door. A few steps away from the car, a cat streaked past her from out of nowhere. Abigail let out a small yelp of surprise. This time she could tell it was a cat from the motion sensor activated lights that had turned on when she pulled up to the house. She was almost certain that it was the same size and shape as the animal from the road.

"Devil cat!" Abigail shook her fist in the direction the cat had disappeared in, toward the wooden fence around the property. "Out to get me!" She knew she wasn't being rational with that last part. But it somehow felt personal to have that happen twice on her way to her house and she felt strangely safer now that she was inside, her back against the door. She flicked on the light switch.

The gray blur Abigail encountered was indeed the same one that darted across the road in the light from her car's headlights. It was a slim, seal-point Siamese cat. He sat under the lowest log of the fence, his tail curled around his forepaws and his whiskers twitching. The tip of his tail lightly tapped the snow as he stared at the house with intense blue eyes.

"Meow," he said. *She's boooommmee.*

A fluffy, ginger cat stepped out from the shadow of the fence, her long, wispy fur shimmered in the moonlight. Her long whiskers and tufted ears twitched slightly, her tail curved around her legs as she sat beside the Siamese and fixed her amber eyes on the house.

"Meow," she said. *So is he-ee.*

They were joined by an enormous, dark-furred Norwegian Forest Cat. He was stockier than either of them, with a thickly furred neck and broad chest which made him seem like a bear cub compared to his more delicate companions. He sat himself by the other flank of the Siamese, his yellow eyes focused unblinking on the house. His silence only emphasized the enormity of his presence. The Siamese and Ginger cat joined him in sitting in silence. The air around them was filled with expectation.

Chapter Two

Abigail's hands trembled as she tossed the ingredients of her dinner – a green smoothie – into the blender. She pressed down on the lid and hit the appropriate button. Holding onto the countertop, Abigail took a deep breath, closing her eyes. The sound of the blender's motor sputtering caused her to open her eyes and lift her head up to see the lights flickering.

"What now?" Abigail stared at the blender, confused. *Was it shorting out?*

"It can't be happening. It's brand new!" She growled with angry disbelief, almost as if challenging the kitchen appliance to try something again. The lights stopped flickering. The blender completed its cycle before shutting itself off.

"Very wise." After unplugging the machine, Abigail filled her favorite tumbler with her smoothie and went to take a sip. That was when the lights started to flicker again. Could this be a brown out? She left the kitchen to peer outside. She moved to the nearest window. At the drapery's movement, two cats scattered into the shadows. Abigail gazed up to see snow slowly falling from the sky. If anything, the weather was getting better. Abigail furrowed her brows at what she saw: the cat that had nearly killed her on the road not long ago, sitting under her fence and looking at her like nothing had happened. The audacity! Fuming, Abigail shut the drapes and spun around, ready to return to the kitchen - only to see Jacob Morris standing right there! She didn't remember dropping the tumbler as she clutched her hands to her chest and screamed. Then she snatched an old book from the table beside her and threw it, watching as it sailed through his ghostly body and slid across the hardwood floor.

"I know you've always hated surprises, Abigail. But that is no excuse for throwing classic books at my head,"Jacob said, apparently unfazed by the attempted assault. "Good shot, by the way. I'm impressed. But I'm also insulted. Is that anyway to greet your dearly departed friend and business partner?"

Abigail paced around the room. "This isn't happening. Jacob is dead. I was at the funeral. I went to the internment. You can't be here."

"Well, I certainly can't be here in the flesh, as you are right, I'm dead."

Abigail shook her head. "No. No. No. No. No! You are just some figment of my imagination. Some kind of stress-related hallucination. You are a product of my subconscious. You are not real. This isn't happening."

"You can say that all you want. It doesn't change the fact that it is. Right now." Jacob smiled at her and sat down in the chair by the fireplace. It has always been his favorite place to sit and talk. The room was filled with the scent of wood smoke. Underneath it was a faint smell of ozone, like a distant thunderstorm. Abigail scowled at the specter sitting in the chair. A lanky man with an easy smile. There was a blue hue to his body and a shimmer of white light encircling it. The answer popped into her head.

"Of course! I'm in a coma thanks to that stupid cat! When I slammed on the breaks I didn't just skid off to the side of the road. It must have been much, much worse. I probably hit a tree. The car is a write off and I'm still sitting there slowly freezing to death because no one ever comes out this way." Abigail turned and glared at the window, as if she could send her anger out at the cat she suspected was still sitting out there.

"Don't be ridiculous, Abigail." Jacob could only shake his head. "You're fine. You didn't have an accident. You're not in a coma. You made it home safe and sound." Jacob stopped and considered what he just said. "That sounds strange, even though I gave you this place in my will."

"Yeah, well, it's been strange living out here." Abigail turned back to Jacob. "But I can see why you loved the place. I never meant to stay. I was only supposed to be here for a month, maybe two, while everything got sorted out. But everyone who wanted to buy it wanted to change it. I just couldn't bring myself to sell it."

"I appreciate that." Jacob pointed his finger and winked at her the way he always used to. Was he truly there? Or was he only some delusion her brain had cooked up to try and help her cope with the Christmas season. Her brain had a very odd idea of what was helpful, if that was the case.

"But don't get too comfortable here," Jacob continued. "That's why the Cats and I are here. To warn you."

"Cats? As in plural?"

"Funny how that's the part of what I just said to you that you focused on." Jacob shook his head. "Yes, plural. We are here to warn you, Abigail."

"About what, exactly?" Abigail was beginning to doubt this was an actual ghost sitting in front of her.

"About your own untimely demise, my dear." Jacob looked Abigail in the eyes. It sent a chill of terror through her body. She had never seen that kind of emotion in Jacob's eyes before. It was as if he had seen it happen.

"Are you sure I'm not in a coma?" Abigail whispered.

"Yes. For now, you are safe and sound, if a little overworked by your boss."

"I'm the boss." Abigail was not amused.

"Exactly. You make the big choices in your business. But you've been neglecting the important things in your life. I admit I was wrong about the Connecticut connection, but that doesn't mean you have to become a hermit. There are people around you that are supporting you in ways you don't even begin to fathom, especially during this magical Christmas season. But even kindness has its limits, they won't stick around forever. You need to wake up to how the choices you've been making are affecting you and those around you. If you keep on the path you've been going down, you don't have much time left."

"I see now," Abigail pointed her index finger to the ceiling. "This is all because I went to visit your grave this morning. Then I was thinking about how I used to come and visit you out in the car a few minutes ago. And now, here you are!" She spread her arms out in an imitation of a game show host showing the grand prize to the contestants.

"Wrong. You don't see at all. So the cats and I have our work cut out for us, trying to get you to open your eyes and truly see."

"Again with the cats. You never had pets. Why do you keep mentioning these cats."

"They're going to visit you."

"No!"

"I'm afraid you don't have any more choice in the matter than I do."

"Why are you here, Jacob?"

"Haven't you been listening at all?!" Jacob's voice became deeper and echoed through the house.

"I mean, why are you here now? If it isn't because I visited your grave or was thinking about our visits here out in the car, why are you here?"

Jacob settled back in the chair and nodded. "Fair enough. I didn't make that clear. We are here because it is the Christmas season. It is a magical time of year. You know I always believed that. But that belief wasn't enough to compensate for the important things that I neglected through the course of my life. My misdeeds have stayed with me and this is part of my recompense for them."

"Surely this is extreme for your misdeeds. I know you weren't a saint in life, Jacob. But you never killed anyone. You never deliberately harmed anyone. Neither have I. Why are the otherworldly powers that be doing this to you? Why are you doing this to me?!"

"We aren't only accountable for the things we do, but for the things we had the opportunity to do but turned a blind eye to, saying 'it's not my problem, someone else will take care of it.' I had the opportunity to do so much more for my fellow human beings while I was alive. I had more than enough money, even with what I squandered here and there, to do much more for many more people. Now that I'm dead, I can do nothing. Nothing but watch the suffering of those I cared about most in life."

"Jacob. . ." Abigail didn't know how to respond.

"So, the otherworldly powers that be, as you so neatly put it, have decided, in their benevolence, to send me, along with the three Cats of Christmas, to give you the chance to open your eyes and course correct."

"Three cats? But I've already nearly been killed by one of them. That should mean that I only have two left. No, there was the one outside the house, too. That makes two. So there should only be one cat left."

Jacob couldn't hide the laughter that bubbled up as he said: "You're still not getting it." He cleared his throat, putting on a serious face. "You will receive a visit from the first Cat of Christmas at 1 a.m. on December 23rd. The second Cat of Christmas will come by at 1 a.m. on the 24th, and the third one at 1 a.m. on Christmas Day."

"Couldn't they all happen on the same night?"

"Abigail," Jacob gave an exasperated sigh and pinched the bridge of his spectral nose. "Be grateful that you are being given this much time. And that they have chosen to give you this chance at all. It's one I was never given." Jacob peered back up into Abigail's eyes. The expression of sadness in his eyes made Abigail inhale a sharp breath. She looked down at her hands and nodded.

"Good!" Jacob seemed to cheer up at Abigail's resignation to the visits. "You've best get yourself ready. One a.m. will be here before you know it." The ghost of Jacob Morris got up from the chair and faded from view, leaving behind a faint scent of ozone in the air.

Ethan Clarke sat on the edge of the bed in his room at The Nell, a cozy inn in the heart of Little Dickens, where every nook and cranny was adorned with whimsical Christmas decorations. The room exuded the enchanting spirit of the season, with a meticulously decorated Christmas tree trimmed with twinkling lights, colorful ornaments, and fragrant pine needles.

Soft, golden light emanated from a vintage-style lamp on the bedside table, casting a warm, holiday glow which danced with the room's festive ambiance. Making the tinsel and garlands hung around the room sparkle with even more magic.

Outside the window, a gentle snowfall painted the town in a pristine blanket of white, turning Little Dickens into a winter wonderland straight out of a holiday postcard.

Ethan held his phone, the screen illuminating his face with cold blue light. A text conversation was open with a contact named "BOSS."

BOSS: How did it go with Carson?

Ethan hesitated for a moment before typing his response.

ETHAN: No luck. She's adamant about not selling.

Almost immediately, his phone buzzed with a reply.

BOSS: Use that Clarke charm! We need that deal closed by year-end.

Ethan let out a soft, humorless chuckle before typing back.

ETHAN: Charm is not going to cut it with her. She's committed to her values and vision.

Another quick response from his boss.

BOSS: It's about the numbers. Push the offer.

Ethan's fingers hesitated over the keyboard, his brow furrowing.

ETHAN: It's not just about numbers for her, Uncle. She sees through our tactics.

There was a brief pause before his phone lit up again.

BOSS: Uncle?? Remember, professionalism at all times. We can't afford slip-ups.

Ethan bit his lip, realizing his mistake, and quickly typed a response.

ETHAN: Sorry. I meant, it's a lost cause. She won't budge.

His phone buzzed again.

BOSS: Persistence, Ethan. Keep at it. Make her see the benefits.

Ethan sighed and set his phone down, staring out the window. Across the street, the inviting lights of Margot's Cocoa Cafe beckoned with promises of steaming hot cocoa topped with marshmallows, freshly baked gingerbread cookies, and the comforting aroma of holiday spices. As he leaned back against the headboard, he reached for the remote control on the nightstand and turned on the TV. The familiar scenes of "Home Alone 2: Lost in New York" filled the room, and he couldn't help but smile when Kevin lip synced "Merry Christmas, you filthy animal."

Ethan felt a mix of frustration and futility creep back into him, knowing too well the challenge that lay ahead of him. He was miles away from the holiday hustle he was used to, assigned to this snowy small-town that couldn't decide what century it was in.

THE CAT OF

CHRISTMAS

PAST

Chapter Three

The encounter with Jacob down by the fireplace of his former home had rattled Abigail so she didn't get any of the work done she had brought home with her. Instead of trying to do anything and risk sounding like a deranged lunatic that thought she was visited by her deceased business partner, Abigail decided to call it a day and went to bed much earlier than she normally would have. If she had been thinking more clearly - which how could she possibly be while talking with a person who died last year? - the idea of being interrupted in her work by a cat would have struck her as absurd. One in the morning was nothing when working from home late.

The bed was the only place Abigail knew to find any comfort. Maybe it was sleep deprivation, along with stress. She just needed a good night's sleep and it would be as if nothing happened. Abigail crawled into bed and laid there, looking at the ceiling. She covered her face with her hands. "What a nightmare!" She let out a groan. Then she dropped her hands and let out a snort of derisive laughter. Was this what she had been reduced to? Her life was such a nightmare that she needed to go to sleep to escape it? She wasn't about to get out of bed now. She didn't know what she was going to do in the morning. Now she needed to go to sleep, she could figure out tomorrow when it got here. Abigail reached over to the lamp on her night stand and tapped the bottom to turn it off.

Abigail jolted awake, her gaze fixed on the darkness. She held her breath, listening carefully for what had awoken her. The light on her nightstand blinked on and off, illuminating the room then plunging it back into darkness. There was too much of a gap between the turning on and off for it to be like when Jacob appeared. He said something about a cat showing up at one in the morning. Did she actually think that would happen? She wondered if her mind was playing tricks on her, making her think the light was turning on and off. Was it all part of her imagination?

Abigail slowly turned her head to see a faint glow coming from the nightstand. Her eyes widened as she saw the fluffiest ginger cat she had ever laid eyes on, sitting on top of the bedside table. It seemed to be surrounded by a scent that was a reminder of days long gone, like the pages of a cherished, well-worn book. As the cat batted the lamp base, the room was plunged into darkness again and a hint of a Christmas carol floated through the air. Abigail sat up and reached over to touch the lamp base, turning the light back on.

"Hey!" she yelled at the cat. "What are you doing in here?! Get out!" She jumped out of bed when the ginger cat hopped down from the bedside table to the floor. She stepped into her slippers and advanced toward the cat in an intimidating manner.

"Scram!" She frantically waved her hands, trying to indicate for the cat to get out. Sure enough, it quickly scampered away from her bedroom in a hurry, leaving a faint trail of holiday magic behind. Abigail slumped back onto her bed in relief.

"What am I doing?" She asked herself. "I don't want that cat in here."

Abigail marched out of her bedroom, determined to catch the ginger cat. She flicked on every light switch as she went along, creating a wide path of illumination in order to spot the feline intruder. The game of hide-and-seek began as Abigail searched for the fluffy cat around the house. She looked under the couch, in between furniture and even checked inside cabinets for any signs of its presence. She didn't know whose pet it was, it didn't have an identifying collar around its neck.

But it could be microchipped, a voice in her head said. Why? She didn't have the supplies necessary for keeping a cat to take to the vet in the morning to be checked for a microchip. No, the cat was going back outside where it came from.

"I've got you now!" Abigail yelled gleefully when she had the cat trapped. She reached out to scoop it up, but the fur was so soft that she misjudged her hold, and the ginger cat slipped through her grasp, leaving a whisper of vanilla and old-fashioned candles behind. It darted between her legs and ran upstairs, causing Abigail to nearly lose her balance and stumble into a corner of her kitchen cabinets.

"No! Come back here!" She held onto the edge of the kitchen counter to steady herself before taking off after the cat up the stairs. When she reached the top, she scanned the hallway until she saw a flash of movement coming from her bedroom. She slowly tiptoed up to the doorway and peered around the corner. The ginger cat was there, staring right at her. Abigail lunged towards it, but it managed to get away in the knick of time. She ended up face down on the bed, looking like Superman flying across the room. "Ughn! I give up!"

The ginger cat jumped onto the windowsill. It sat there looking at Abigail. Abigail lifted her head up from her comforter to see the ginger cat sitting there. She pushed herself up and positioned herself so she was sitting on the side of the bed. "Ha! So that's how you got in!" She spotted that the window was open and the light but cold breeze was causing the draperies to flutter.

"Meow." said the ginger cat. *Naturally. Now, if you will follow me, you have a lot to see before we are done.* She stood up and turned toward the open window.

"Of course!" Abigail threw her arms up in the air in exasperation. "Of course you'd leave on your own. If I'd known that, I wouldn't have bothered chasing you all around my house."

The ginger cat stared back at Abigail. Abigail sat on the bed, waiting for the ginger cat to jump back out the window.

"Well, go on. Get out of here!" Abigail said when the ginger cat didn't move.

"All right, then." Abigail said, rising to her feet. "I'll just have to take you out the front door." She bent and reached the cat. This time it didn't slip through her fingers. As her fingertips touched its soft, fluffy fur, the ginger cat appeared to emit a warm light, followed by a blinding flash of illumination that seemed to emanate from its body, enveloping them both in a cocoon of Christmas enchantment.

"What just happened?" Abigail released the ginger cat from her arms and looked around, ignoring its indignant meow as it hit the ground. "This isn't my house! What's going on?" She asked no one in particular, turning to the ginger cat who arched its back at her and hissed, the sound harmonizing with distant jingle bells. "Well, that is extremely unhelpful." Abigail turned and looked around at the house she was now standing in. It wasn't her house, yet there was something that stirred a sense of familiarity within her.

"Smooooo-kyyy!" A young girl's voice called from another room in the house. The sound of the voice and the name it called out caused Abigail's eyes to widen in disbelief and she whirled around to hiss at the ginger cat.

"You didn't! It can't be!"

"Smoooo-kyyy! Where are you?" The voice was closer now, accompanied by the soft chimes of a Christmas song playing in the background. And a ten year old Abigail walked into the room, her eyes sparkling with the joy of the holiday season. Abigail gasped when she saw her, and backed away from her younger self.

"Meow," said the Cat of Christmas Past. *Don't worry, she can't see you. Or hear you. She can't even hear me meow.* And the ginger cat sat right in front of the young Abigail and meowed up at her. The young girl ignored the ginger cat, caught up in her search for Smoky.

"Stop that!" Abigail said to the Cat of Christmas Past. "You made your point." She turned and followed her younger self around the house, the air filled with the scent of freshly baked Christmas cookies. It was obvious that it was Christmas time. Abigail knew she was ten because that was the Christmas . . .

"I'm asleep. I'm still asleep. This is all just a stress-induced dream. I'm dreaming this because that cat nearly killed me out on the road. This is how my brain is processing it all. That stupid cat!"

The Cat of Christmas Past let out a sharp meow, it's fur shimmering with holiday magic. *Watch what you say about my friend!*

"Bah, humbug!" Abigail snapped at the cat. "That cat is what triggered this. I haven't – I forgot all about- I never wanted to think about this ever again. And now here I am in a nightmare, stuck watching my younger self go through it all again. Thank you, oh so much, for this Christmas trip down memory lane."

The younger Abigail stood up after checking under the couch. "Come on, Smoky. This isn't funny. You're going to miss all the fun seeing what Santa brought us for Christmas!"

"Abigail! Honey!"

Abigail started and turned her head at the sound of her mother's voice calling her younger self from downstairs.

"Yes, Mommy?" Young Abigail called down to her mother.

"It's time to open presents. Don't you want to see what Santa brought you?"

"I can't find Smoky, Mommy. Smoky can't miss Christmas. I told him all about it."

From where she was standing at the bannister along the hall, Abigail could see and hear what she hadn't as her younger self. Her mother speaking to her step-father Jim, who stood in the doorway of the living room, wearing a Santa hat. *Coward.* Abigail's expression contorted in contempt at the sight of him. The Cat of Christmas Past crouched down and growled. Abigail nodded her approval. "You got that right."

"I told you she would notice!" Abigail's mother was saying.

Jim shrugged in response. "She'll get over it. She'll see the presents and forget all about that stupid cat." Abigail winced, remembering her careless words.

The Cat of Christmas Past looked up at her. "Meow." *Well?*

"I'm sorry, I hear now how bad that sounded." The ginger cat slow blinked her eyes at Abigail and turned back to the scene unfolding before them. Ten year old Abigail started descending the stairs, radiating anticipation.

"Oh, honey," her mom said, placing her hands on young Abigail's shoulders. "Don't worry about Smoky. Smoky is okay.."

"You know where he is?" Young Abigail looked down at her mother, eyes full of hope.

"Honey, Smoky's found himself a new home. One where there isn't someone allergic to him."

Both Abigails glanced towards the living room doorway, but Jim wasn't there anymore.

"Abigail," her mother said to call back her attention. "Look at me. I know you liked Smoky-"

"It was Smoky's home first!' Young Abigail stamped her foot on the stair in protest. "It's not fair!"

"No, what's not fair is that I had to choose between Jim, the man I love, and your cat." Young Abigail's mother tightened her grip on her shoulders. "But that was a choice I had to make. Can't you be a big girl for your mommy? Can you try to understand that Jim makes Mommy happy? You want Mommy to be happy, don't you?"

Young Abigail nodded. "Yes, Mommy."

"Good, now give me a Christmas hug." Abigail hugged her mother.

"Now," her mother held out her hand for Abigail to hold. "Let's go open our Christmas presents, huh?" Young Abigail took her mother's hand and went down the last few stairs to stand at her mother's side. They walked into the living room holding hands. Abigail and the Cat of Christmas Past went down the stairs and into the living room after them. In the living room, they watched Abigail's mother and step-father ooh and ah over the presents as they were unwrapped. Abigail walked over to the fireplace mantle and looked at the family pictures on it. There were pictures of Abigail and her older brother Andrew at the beach with their mother. There was Andrew's high school graduation picture. The ginger cat jumped onto the mantle and weaved through the pictures, almost knocking some over. Abigail picked up her brother's graduation picture, a bittersweet smile playing on her lips.

"I can't blame him for not coming home that Christmas. He hated Jim more than I did. He was older and was used to his freedom. When Jim tried to be head of the household and tell Andrew what to do, it drove him crazy." She put the picture back on the mantle. She turned back to watch her ten-year-old self sitting there at the foot of the Christmas tree pretending to be engrossed with the presents so she didn't have to interact with her mother or Jim.

"This was the second worst Christmas in my life." She leaned against the fireplace and crossed her arms. The Cat of Christmas Past jumped onto her crossed arms and there was a glow of illumination coming from its furry form. There was a flash of light, brighter than a Christmas star, as the Cat of Christmas Past enveloped them both in a cocoon of Christmas enchantment.

Abigail's eyes widened as the Cat of Christmas Past whisked them away from her childhood home, enveloping them in a swirl of vanilla-scented Christmas magic. This new house was also recognizably familiar, as it was yet another place she'd cast away to the recesses of her memory—one that she hadn't wanted to recall. Her expression changed to one of distress as painful memories resurfaced.

"This is Andrew's house." Abigail said to the ginger cat who was still in her arms. Abigail walked over to the large mantle and fireplace, hung with two regular sized stockings and one smaller, adorned with festive Christmas decorations.

"This was seven years later." Tears threatened to spill out of her eyes as she walked from one end to the other, taking in all the pictures: Andrew's graduation from College, a photo from Andrew and Marcie's wedding, and many pictures of her brother, his wife and their baby, Charlie. Charlie's first birthday.

"Said the little lamb to the shepherd boy . . ."

Abigail turned around to see herself, a young woman, with two year old Charlie in her arms, singing softly to him, walking over to the Christmas Tree, the ornaments reflecting the soft glow of Christmas lights.

"Mommy and Daddy should be home from the Christmas party soon. Yes, they will. And we can tell them all about the milk and cookies that you got ready to put out for Santa."

Little Charlie reached out and tried to grab one of the shiny, round ornaments from the branches. Laughing, Abigail stepped back from the tree. Both Abigails turned their heads to look at the door when someone knocked sharply on it. Past Abigail was hesitant.

"Who could that be?" She looked out the window and saw a police car parked outside on the street. Feeling like she couldn't breathe, she held Charlie closer and went to the door. She opened it to find a policeman in his thirties standing on the porch. "H-hello, officer. What is it?"

"Are you Abigail Carson?" The officer asked, eyes flickering to Charlie before looking back at her.

"Yes. What's happened? Why are you here?" Past Abigail's terror at what the officer was going to say grew with each second that passed.

"Oh!" Abigail groaned, "Don't play dumb, girl! You know exactly what he's doing here! You know exactly what happened, you just don't want to admit it!"

The Cat of Christmas Past gazed up at Abigail. "Meow." *She's scared. You're scared. It's okay to be afraid for your brother, his wife and for Charlie.*

"Your brother and his wife have been in an accident."

"Are they going to be okay?"

The officer shook his head, looking at Charlie again. "It doesn't look good. I've come to take you and the baby to the hospital. Please come with me, miss."

"Yes, of course. Right away." Past Abigail grabbed her coat and purse, Charlie's little coat and boots and followed the officer out to the car. She'd put everything on them on their way to the hospital.

Abigail remained on the porch, holding the Cat of Christmas Past in her arms, as her younger self and Charlie got in the back of the police car. The officer then got in behind the wheel and drove away.

"This was the worst Christmas of my life." Abigail's voice quivered with the weight of Christmas memories.

The ginger cat looked up at Abigail. "Meow." *Let's go to the hospital.* A blinding light emitted from inside the cat, the Christmas magic intensifying.

Abigail found herself standing in the intensive care unit waiting room, the hospital was adorned with Christmas decorations, the twinkling lights offering cold comfort as she was met with the sight of her younger self sitting with her two-year old nephew Charlie. He was asleep, his little body slumping against the chair beside her. Her younger self looked down at him, the worried expression on her face making her seem much older than she was.

"I was right to be worried. I was so glad that he was asleep. I don't know what I would have said to him if he had asked me-"

Abigail was interrupted by the entrance of a man in his late thirties. The man was dressed in a crisp and tailored suit, his hair cut short and neat with a slight sheen to it. He had an air of authority and control about him as he moved, his eyes focused and intent on the nurses' station ahead of him. He strode over to the nurses' station with purpose and focus.

"I received a call that Andrew Carson and his wife Marcia Carson were brought in here. Is there any word on their status?"

"Are you a member of the family, sir?" the nurse said, looking the man standing before her up and down.

"No, I'm Andrew's supervisor. I -"

"Jacob Morris?" Abigail's younger self had got up and taken a few steps toward the nurses' station.

"Yes," the man turned at the sound of his name. Past Abigail was nervous about meeting Andrew's boss. She held out her hand, "I'm Abigail."

Jacob shook her prooffered hand. "Abigail, thank you for calling me. Any news?"

She shook her head and gestured towards the intensive care unit doors. "No changes since we arrived. They're still in critical condition."

Jacob ran his hands through his hair. "I just can't believe this. I was with them two hours ago at the Christmas party."

"None of it feels real. Thankfully, Charlie fell asleep half an hour after we got here. I don't know if he understands everything that's going on."

Jacob and Past Abigail then walked over to where Charlie was sleeping.

"Why is it always the best people that things like this happen to? Andrew is the best person I've ever met."

Abigail's younger self had been keeping herself together until she heard Jacob say that. She struggled to keep back a sob. Her voice trembled a bit as she took a shaky breath.

"He really is."

"No, I mean it." Jacob put a hand on Abigail's younger self's shoulder. "He puts me to shame."

"Andrew's always talking about how business savvy you are."

"And he never stops talking about his clever sister who's going to college. I wish we were meeting under better circumstances."

"Me too," she said before they slipped into a companionable silence.

"I want to leave *now*, cat." Abigail said. The Cat of Christmas Past did not respond. The doors to the intensive care unit began opening, the sound alerted Abigail to the urgency of her situation. "I said I want to leave. *Now!*" Still the cat remained silent. The doors opened wider, and two doctors entered the waiting room, their white coats in stark contrast with the Christmas decorations.

"Miss Carson?" one of the doctors asked.

Abigail's younger self nodded. The expressions on both doctor's faces were enough for her to know what they were going to say before a single word was spoken out loud. It was as if she were back in the hospital waiting room once again, suffocating under its weight. She watched as her younger self crumbled into the chair beside Charlie. The scent of vanilla and the forest grew stronger as a burst of light emanated from the cat, enveloping them in a cocoon of Christmas magic.

Chapter Four

Abigail was so relieved to no longer be in the hospital waiting room, she didn't bother to berate the ginger cat for not getting them out of there when she had demanded it to, the scent of hospital antiseptic slowly fading from her senses.

"So, now where are we?" She glanced around them. The Cat of Christmas Past jumped from Abigail's arms and began walking down the hallway adorned with subtle Christmas decorations. After a moment, it stopped and looked back to find Abigail still rooted in place.

"Meow." *We have to go this way to see this event of your past.* The Cat of Christmas Past turned and started down the hall again.

"Oh, so I have to follow you now? Fine." Abigail hurried to catch up with the cat. She didn't know how this worked if it *wasn't* a product of her over-tired, over-stressed mind, which it was looking more and more like it wasn't. What if she lost the cat, would she be stuck in this nightmare forever? She shuddered at the thought and stuck close to the ginger cat. It had reached the end of the hallway, where a wooden door was closed. The cat looked back at her, waiting.

Abigail looked down at the cat. "So, you can go through time but you can't walk through doors? Is that it? You need me to open it for you?"

"Meow." *Don't be silly, of course I can walk through doors. You don't think that you can, though. So I thought you might feel better opening the door.*

With that, the Cat of Christmas Past walked through the closed door. Abigail stood there in silence for a moment, stunned. Then she panicked and tugged on the door handle. It wouldn't open. Abigail started to bang on the door.

"Hey! Cat! Wait! I can't get the door open."

The Cat of Christmas Past, well, the front half of her, appeared through the door. "Meow." And she disappeared back through the door.

"What?! Well, that's easy for you to say." Abigail threw her hands up in the air and leaned against the door. The pressure of her weight opened the door and Abigail nearly toppled to the floor. She caught herself in time and used the momentum to swing herself around to see inside the room. It was the College's auditorium, beautifully decorated for Christmas. It was one of the rare Christmas graduations. There were only five of them, Abigail included, and they were all graduating early because they had business placements for the new year. They were all standing on the stage in their caps and gowns, the Christmas lights illuminating the event with a festive glow. The lack of pomp and circumstance was the trade off for getting a head start on life. Or so Jacob had told her. He was hard to miss in the small group of spectators in the auditorium.

Abigail sank into one of the cushioned auditorium seats, grateful to sit. She hadn't realized how drained reliving all these memories had left her. The Cat of Christmas Past leaped up on her lap, its fur radiating a warm, soothing Christmas glow.

"Meow?" *How's this, is it a better memory?*

"This was an okay Christmas. I wish Andrew could've seen me. He would've been so proud. His little sister, following in his footsteps." She watched as her younger self, diploma in hand, descended the stairs and walked over to where Jacob was waiting. Both of them were all smiles.

"When was the last time I smiled like that?" Abigail asked herself.

"Congratulations, Abigail! You did it!"

"I did it!"

"Now, let's go celebrate. I want to introduce you to everyone at the Christmas party."

"You must be the last company around that still has Christmas parties. No one else seems to be having them anymore."

"Going the way of the dinosaur, so I'm told. But, you know me. I'm old and set in my ways. There'll always be a Christmas party, as long as I'm around."

Laughing, the two of them exited through the door Abigail had recently come through.

Abigail looked at the ginger cat laying on her lap. "I guess we're going to a party."

"Meow." *If you insist.* A flash of light engulfed Abigail and the cat, the scent of vanilla and the forest intensified.

The small office was filled with the enchanting smell of mulled cider and spiced cookies, their aromatic tendrils dancing through the air, enticing everyone's senses. The lights on the Christmas tree were as bright as stars, and the ornaments glowed with a warm, festive radiance. People bustled around, their cheerful chatter filling the room, dressed in vibrant, holiday-themed clothing, and Abigail felt a wave of nostalgia for a simpler time.

"I forgot how humble the beginnings of Morris and Carson Developments were." Abigail said as she dodged the white paper chain, hanging from the drop-down ceiling, the Cat of Christmas Past was batting around, its movements adding to the merriment of the atmosphere. No one seemed to take notice. Every eye was on a younger Jacob wearing a Santa hat jauntily angled on his head. She couldn't remember now whether someone else had plopped the hat on his head or if he'd done it himself. It was the kind of thing he could pull off.

"Welcome, everyone. Welcome to the first annual Christmas party of Morris Developments." There was much cheering and clapping that followed these words, the festive spirit in the room contagious. Jacob paused until everyone calmed down.

"Now, it's not much right now. But it's what we could afford for our first year in business. And I couldn't be happier to have had the opportunity to introduce you all to our newest employee, Abigail Carson." The room erupted into cheers and clapping again. Abigail - in her past form - wore her graduation cap but had changed out of the gown into the most festive thing she owned: a red sweater. She stood beside Past Jacob and waved at the crowd.

"Good thing I was too excited to be starting this job to notice those two women giving me death stares." Abigail muttered to the Cat of Christmas Past. "If looks could kill. Yikes!"

"I'm happy that Abigail could join us here today for this Christmas Party," Jacob continued. "Because I want to dedicate it to the memory of the person who embodied the spirit of Christmas more than anybody I ever met: Abigail's late brother, Andrew Carson."

Abigail watched her past self's surprised reaction. She watched herself mouth the words "Thank you" to Jacob.

"What else could I do? That was unexpected. And I'm sure it was meant to be a kind gesture. But it was kind of weird, to me, anyway. But, hey, it's his company, who's going to say anything?" Abigail shrugged at the Cat of Christmas Past. She stole a glance over at the two women who had been glaring at her past self. She felt a sense of vindication wash over her as they had the decency to stare down at their drinks in embarrassment after Jacob's announcement.

The Cat of Christmas Past's meow was followed by a flash of light, and they embarked on the next part of their journey, a sense of merriment and camaraderie in the air.

"Welcome everyone, once again to the Morris and Carson Development Christmas Gala on behalf of the Little Dickens Hospital-" As Jacob, much older than before, began his speech at the Little Dickens Country Club, Abigail surveyed her surroundings, the grandeur of the gala filling the air with a sense of enchantment and elegance.

"This is the Christmas Gala from a few years ago. Why are we here? It's practically yesterday. What's the point?"

"Meow." *The past is the past.* The Cat of Christmas Past answered before lifting her fluffy, ginger tail and gracefully walking away, her scent of vanilla and the forest intermingling with the atmosphere.

"No, wait. Get back here!" Abigail chased after the ginger cat through the milling crowd and dancers on the dance floor. She lunged for the ginger cat at one of the nearby tables covered in wine-colored cloth, but almost ended up face-planting under it instead. The cat had wriggled away from her grasp. Abigail felt embarrassed to have been caught crawling out from underneath the table, until she realized that no one could see or hear her—or the cat. After brushing her hair out of her eyes, she studied the room for any sign of the feline. It was gone.

In front of where she had emerged from under the table, stood a man she recognized all too well.

"Oh, no. We're in that one." Abigail facepalmed when she saw Jacob guiding her slightly younger self over to where the tall, attractive man was standing. His jet black hair swept back to highlight the fine features- a sharp nose, strong jawline and chiseled chin. The electric blue eyes that she would later discover were courtesy of contact lenses. He was wearing a classic all-black suit with a festive hint of red coming from his cumberbund.

"Wallace?" Jacob said, his guest turning and smiling back at him.

"Jacob! Wonderful party. Thank you for the invitation." He shook Jacob's outstretched hand.

"Thanks for coming. I hope you've had the chance to see what Little Dickens has to offer."

"I've only caught a brief glimpse." Wallace told them, his eyes darting over to Abigail. "But if what I've seen is anything to go by, I think maybe I'm beginning to understand what you see in this town."

"Are you?" Past Abigail said, genuinely surprised. "Then maybe you can explain it to me because I've never understood it."

"Where are my manners?" Jacob turned to Past Abigail. "Abigail Carson, I'd like to introduce you to Wallace Covemoor. Wallace, Abigail Carson, the Carson of Morris and Carson Developments."

Past Abigail held out her satin-gloved hand for a handshake but instead of shaking it, to their surprise Wallace kissed it in a gesture of old-world charm.

"It's a pleasure to finally meet you, Abigail. Jacob has been very tight-lipped about you during our meetings back home."

"And where is home for you, Wallace?" Past Abigail asked, subconsciously tossing her hair back over her shoulder, a playful glint in her eyes.

"Connecticut. There's nothing quite like it at Christmas time."

"I'll take your word for it."

The strains of Elvis's Blue Christmas started playing over the sound system.

"The King is one of my favorites." Wallace said to Past Abigail. "May I have this dance?" Past Abigail was a little surprised and looked over at Jacob. When she saw him smiling she became suspicious about this seemingly innocent introduction. She accepted Wallace's offer anyway and they stepped out onto the dance floor.

"I knew Jacob was too happy about the whole thing. He really did set me up!" Abigail said to the ginger cat, who had reappeared on top of the table beside her.

"Meow." *Almost there.* The Cat of Christmas Past brushed up against Abigail and with another flash of light they were transported to the patio of the Country Club. Abigail from two years ago is looking elegant in a blue gown with white opera gloves and Wallace Covemoor is dapper in a gray suit with a red bow tie and matching cumberbund. The patio of the Country Club is decorated with sparkling lights and festive decorations. The air hummed with the strains of Christmas music.

"I can't believe it's already been a year since we met. Right here at this Christmas party." Past Abigail was saying to Wallace.

"I'm so glad that you are wearing the necklace I gave you as an early Christmas present."

"You spoil me." Past Abigail touched the chain of the necklace and she smiled up at Wallace with love in her eyes. The platinum pendant shined like a distant star overhead, sending off slivers of reflected light onto his face. He took his cue from her smile and leaned in to kiss her, their connection deepening in the midst of the festive atmosphere.

"And I'm not done yet. I have another early present for you, Abigail," Wallace said, his eyes gleaming with excitement.

"And here I am making you wait until Christmas morning for yours," Abigail teased.

"Well, this present isn't technically just for you. It's for me, too."

"How so?"

Wallace pulled out a small jewelry box from the inside pocket of his suit jacket. Past Abigail looked from the box to Wallace's face, her heart quickened with anticipation. He opened the box to reveal a ring with an enormous sapphire surrounded by diamonds. He dropped down to one knee.

Past Abigail gasped as she stared at the ring in the box, emotion overwhelming her. "Wallace ... I didn't expect this!"

"I love you, Abigail, and I want to make sure you know it. Will you marry me?" He asked her, still on one knee.

"Yes! Of course I will."

Wallace took the ring from the box and slid it onto her gloved finger. "It's a family heirloom. My family was getting worried that I'd never find someone to wear it. I knew better." Wallace put his hand under Past Abigail's chin and tilted her head up, smiling down at her as he moved closer to kiss her. Past Abigail closed the space between them and wrapped her arms around his shoulders, their lips meeting in a passionate kiss.

When Wallace and Abigail pulled away from each other, they were both beaming from ear to ear. "This has been the best Christmas ever," Abigail said, her voice filled with joy. She gazed down at her ring, a symbol of their love and the promise of a beautiful future together, and smiled.

Wallace put his arm around her waist and they began to walk back inside the Country Club.

Abigail stood there watching as they made their way through the crowd of guests. Everyone had observed the engagement and offered congratulations as they passed by. Exhaling, she glanced down to the ginger cat sitting atop the stone wall that bordered the patio.

"I thought that was the happiest Christmas of my life. It seemed like I had everything. Money, career, a dapper fiance. Look at me now. Standing out here in the snow and cold - in my pajamas - talking to a cat."

"Meow." *Just one left and we're done.* The Cat of Christmas Past tapped Abigail with her fluffy, ginger tail. There was another flash of light.

"I can't believe that you beat me into the office today, Jacob." Past Abigail stood in the doorway of the office, hands on her hips when she saw Jacob sitting at his desk. She crossed the room, taking off her gloves as she walked. "And the morning after your Christmas Gala. You usually don't get back in until the afternoon." She hung her coat up. Met with nothing but silence, she continued. "Did your night cap get tired of waiting for you to finish up counting the money the Gala raised?" Still nothing. She turned around and walked over to Jacob. "Jacob?" She lightly nudged his arm. "This isn't funny-" She caught sight of his phone sitting on the desk. It was flashing notifications of missed calls and texts. Jacob never let them pile up.

"Ms. Carson?" Susan said. She stood frozen in the doorway. Past Abigail became aware of the fact that she was bent over and holding her hand over her mouth. Seeing Susan snapped her out of the shock.

"I think he's dead, Susan."

"I'll call 911," Susan pulled out her phone and dialed.

"Thank you."

Abigail stood off to the side, shaking with anger. "How could you? This is tied for the worst Christmas of my life!" She glared at the ginger cat and was met with another flash of light. When it cleared again, Abigail saw they were at Jacob's funeral.

"Great! Fantastic! Let's just pop some popcorn and sit back and watch the show, shall we?!?" Abigail glowered down at the Cat of Christmas Past.

"Meow." *None for me, thank you.*

Abigail shook her head then huffed as she folded her arms across her chest and leaned against the wall, surrounded by the soft, muffled sobbing and the low hum of conversations carried on in whispers. She felt the weight of her sorrow pressing into her chest and shoulders as she watched her body sag against Wallace for support. The rustling of coats and the shuffling of feet as people paid respects to the departed Jacob was like white noise in the background.

"Not as big a crowd as I thought there would've been." Wallace was saying. He had his arm around Past Abigail's shoulders.

"It's Christmas Eve, what did you expect? Certainly not for him to die right after his Christmas Gala! People had plans. And Jacob wanted to be buried quickly. It was now or in the new year."

"True. Best to get it out of the way and start the new year fresh. Of course, you'll be selling the business."

Past Abigail turned her head to give her fiance an incredulous look. "He's not even in the ground and you are talking about selling the very thing that was his life!"

"He was married to the business. Soon, you'll be married to me, you won't need that to be your life. Because I'll be it."

"You-what? Are you saying that once we're married you'll be my life?!?!" Past Abigail couldn't believe her ears. Abigail still couldn't believe he'd said that.

"Of course, there'll be the children. But in the beginning, yes."

"Children?!? You never once said anything about having kids. Why bring it up now?!"

"I thought it would cheer you up. I know that its hard to let go, but this chapter of your life has come to an end. You can start a brand new one with me and my family out East."

"Well, it's so very kind of you to let me in on the life you have already planned out from me without asking me once!"

"But I did ask you." Wallace reminded her, taking ahold of Past Abigail's left hand to lift it up in view.

"I stand corrected." Past Abigail extracted her hand from his. She pulled the ring off her finger -"You asked me one time!" - and threw it down the hallway.

"Hey!" Wallace yelled, sprinting after it. He stopped after a few strides and spun around to face her. "That was my great-great-great-grandmother's!You had better not have damaged it!"

"I hope it falls in a vent or something." Past Abigail said under her breath and walked away from Jacob's closed casket.

DECEMBER 23

Chapter Five

Chapter 5: December 23

C Abigail woke to the sound of her alarm blaring. She reached out and silenced it. As she sat up, she looked around, noticing that the lamp was off. She touched it and the room illuminated. Then she looked over at the window: closed like she had left it before going to bed. That means it was all a dream—if the cat had been real, there would have been a draft from an open window and she would be shivering in her bed.

She combed her fingers through her hair, remembering the last few moments before she woke up. "Certainly not one of my finer moments." She threw off the bedsheets and got up. Once she got ready for work, she went down the stairs, turning off lights as she walked by them. She saw the mess in the kitchen. *If I clean it up, it never happened,* she thought to herself. *It won't be there to disturb me when I get back from work.* She picked up the laptop bag from where it had slid off the couch when the cat landed on it while evading her attempts to chase it out of the house. She hadn't had enough energy left after the near miss on the road followed by the ghostly visit from Jacob to do the work she'd planned. Now she had twice as much left to do today.

Abigail was furious. With whom or what, she wasn't sure though she suspected herself. Her rage had been ignited the day before when she'd made the ill-advised decision to visit Jacob's grave. *Spurred on by that headline in the Little Dickens Chronicle,* she reminded herself. She'd never imagined that this single act would set off a chain of events in her life. Who would? In what universe did the ghost of the person whose grave you visited on the date of their death follow you back home? Lunacy. She would never tell a soul about it. She'd wind up in an asylum or something. Which would be a fate worse than marrying Wallace Covemoor. At least then she'd have other housewives to commiserate with. Although she'd scoffed at the thought of becoming a "Real Connecticut Housewife," that holiday special was sounding more appealing now than believing she'd gone mad and was seeing specters and chasing imaginary cats in her dreams.

She took a deep breath as she pulled into her parking spot in the Morris and Carson Developments office. She sat back in the driver's seat and closed her eyes, savoring the feeling of being there. Finally. No ghosts or cats. She opened her eyes and stepped out of the car, laptop bag in hand.

As Abigail stepped out of her car, Ethan Clarke approached with an urgency that matched the brisk morning air. He clutched a manila envelope, the same nervous energy from their last meeting still evident.

"Ethan, what is it?" Abigail asked, slightly exasperated but maintaining her composure.

"Ms. Carson, I need a moment of your time," Ethan said, trying to sound confident.

Abigail, already sensing the topic, replied, "Ethan, we've been over this. Morris and Carson is not for sale."

Ethan kept pace with her as they walked toward the office entrance. "But Ms. Carson, McBane Properties is prepared to make an even more generous offer. The potential benefits are—"

"Generous offers don't change the fact that we're not interested, Ethan," Abigail interjected firmly. "My stance hasn't changed since our last discussion."

Ethan's shoulders sagged, but he still held onto the envelope. "At least consider the proposal, Ms. Carson. For the sake of due diligence."

Abigail stopped, turning to face him squarely. Her tone was laced with a hint of challenge. "Ethan, it's not about due diligence. It's about the vision and integrity of Morris and Carson. McBane's vision and integrity... Let's just say they don't align with ours."

Ethan's confidence waned, the envelope in his hand feeling heavier. "I just thought it was worth considering..."

Abigail nodded, her gaze piercing. "Speaking of due diligence, do you even know who you're working for? What McBane stands for? Consider this: understanding the true nature of who you represent is as important as the deal you're trying to close. Now, if you'll excuse me."

Abigail turned and walked into the building, leaving Ethan standing there staring at the envelope in his hands, grappling with the gap between his ambition and the complex realities of the business world.

Abigail opened the door to the office and stepped in. She had taken two steps toward her desk when the chair turned and revealed Jacob sitting there. Abigail let out a yelp and her laptop bag hit the floor with a loud thud.

Jacob didn't move, or speak. He simply sat there, looking at her with a faint, otherworldly glow. Abigail's heart was pounding in her chest. The sight of Jacob in her office chair sent shivers down her spine, like a ghostly presence straight out of a Christmas ghost story. She backed away, fumbling for the door handle, never taking her eyes off the ghost. But Jacob didn't move to stop her, maintaining an eerie silence.

Susan, curious about the commotion, poked her head around the corner to see what was going on. "What is it, Ms. Carson?" Abigail was staring transfixed at the chair at her desk. Susan couldn't understand why. It was exactly as Abigail left it the afternoon before, except for the red and green ribbon Susan had tied around the backrest.

Abigail wasn't sure she trusted herself to speak. From the look of concern on Susan's face, Abigail could tell that Susan had not seen the chair move or Jacob sitting in it. Why would she? It was Abigail's mind playing tricks on her. She couldn't project it into someone else's reality. Hallucinations, or whatever he was, didn't work that way.

"Is it the tree? It's only until after Christmas. I promise, Ms. Carson. I'll take it down right after."

"The-tree?" Abigail's gaze rested on the three-foot tree on the table between Susan's workstation and her desk, twinkling with Christmas lights and tiny ornaments. If Jacob's ghost hadn't turned her chair around for dramatic effect, she probably would've noticed it sooner. She shook her head and grabbed her laptop bag.

"I'm not in the mood to deal with your holiday touch, Susan. So, fine. As long as it is down right after Christmas, it can stay." She placed her laptop bag on the desk and looked inside to make sure it hadn't been damaged from falling earlier.

"You would not believe the night I had. An animal ran out on the road in front of me and then it just kind of spiraled from there." Abigail looked up to find Susan still watching her with a look of concern. Susan was oblivious to the fact that Jacob's ghost was sitting in the chair waving at her with a grin on his face, knowing full well she didn't see him. "Thank you for your concern, Susan. Is there anything you need?"

"No. Ms. Carson." Susan took a few steps back before turning and hurrying to her workstation.

"Why did you talk to her like that? She's only worried about you."

Abigail turned to the apparition in her chair, putting her hand on her hip. "What are you? My conscience now, too?!" She hissed under her breath. "I can't very well sit down at my desk like I normally would, now can I? How else was I going to end that awkward scene?"

Jacob shrugged, his hands on his lap. "I don't know, but maybe you could've been a bit nicer."

"Why are you still here? Wasn't last night a one and done kind of thing?" Abigail leaned against her desk, arms crossed.

"I suppose it could've been. But, it's been a year since I left the land of the living and . . . " His voice trailed off as he looked at the office door.

"And?"

Jacob looked up at Abigail. "I never thought I'd miss this."

"The business?"

Jacob chuckled and shook his head. "Life. 'I'll rest when I'm dead' I used to say. There truly is no rest for the wicked."

"Come on. You might have cut a few corners here and there. You may not have paid your female staff an equitable wage. But there are people out in the world who have done much worse. Why pick on you? Why pick on me?"

"Always defending me, even when you think I'm a delusion. It makes me wonder if you weren't secretly in love with me."

Abigail arched an eyebrow at the specter. "You were my friend and mentor and you made me partner in this business. I was never romantically interested in you. I thought that went unsaid. But if we're saying the unsaid, are you sure it wasn't the other way around? Because some of the things Wallace said made it sound like it."

"That small-minded whelp," Jacob shook his head again.

"May I remind you that you thought that 'small-minded whelp' was husband material for me?"

"Nobody's perfect. I thought it would be a win-win-win situation. The Covemoor family would gain you, the business would gain from the Covemoor name and you would, I hoped, be happy. I'm sorry that Wallace wasn't what either of us had hoped. But I'm proud of you for not giving up the business to become a Real Connecticut Housewife."

"Ugh. Remind me to never talk to a gravestone ever again." Abigail threw her head back and looked up at

the ceiling.

Jacob laughed.

Susan poked her head into the room, "What was that you said, Ms. Carson?"

Abigail stood up and turned to Susan. "Nothing. I was just realizing all the work that still needs to be done by tomorrow."

"Yes. Ms. Carson. I'm almost finished with the latest revisions."

"Good. I'll look them over this afternoon."

"Yes, Ms. Carson." Susan nodded and returned to her work station.

"That's another thing I'm proud of you for," Jacob nodded his head in Susan's direction. Then the chair was empty. Abigail blinked in surprise. "She's bright, talented and she'll go far." Abigail turned to see Jacob standing by the drafting table, his hands in his pockets, looking at Susan. He shifted so he could see Abigail out of the corner of his eye. "But most of all, she's loyal. Like you." He turned to face Abigail. "You rewarded that loyalty. That's why she hasn't accepted any offers from headhunters for more prestigious jobs in other states on other projects with bigger budgets. She wants to stay and finish this project."

Jacob paused, as though he was listening for something. A huge grin spread over his face. He glanced toward the office door. "And that's not the only reason she's sticking around."

Charlie pushed the office door open and peered in, sliding his body into the room and shutting the door behind him.

"A Christmas tree! Very nice, Aunt Abigail."

"I can't take credit for the tree. It was all Susan's doing." Abigail pointed at Susan in an accusatory manner with the pen she was holding. Charlie shifted his gaze over to Susan, offering her an appreciative smile and nod.

"Festive. It really brightens up the room."

"Thanks, Charlie."

"But . . ." Charlie turned his gaze back to his aunt as he approached her desk. "I didn't see the wreath that I brought you yesterday on the door." He gestured behind him, towards the entrance, where a decorative wreath with red ribbons and golden bells would have been a fitting Christmas decoration. "Did you take it home to hang on your front door?" As he waited for an answer, he rocked on the balls of his feet with his hands clasped together behind his back.

Abigail turned her head to face Susan, who quickly directed her gaze back to the task at hand. Abigail stood up straighter and looked Charlie in the eye. "No. I gave it to the doctors from the Hospital."

Charlie stopped rocking and considered this. "Okkaay. That's something. Maybe you're starting to get into the Christmas spirit, right? Oh! speaking of which," Charlie fumbled inside his winter coat and pulled out two envelopes; one green, one red. "Christmas cards!" He moved closer to his aunt, offering the green envelope. "For you, Aunt Abigail!"

Abigail hesitated for a moment before taking it. She didn't return her nephew's infectious grin, but she couldn't bring herself to refuse the card.

"And for you, Ms. Cardinal," Charlie gave Susan a little bow as he offered her the red envelope.

"Thank you, Charlie." Susan accepted the card and placed it on her desk, even though she wanted to open it then and there. It didn't feel right to open her card when Abigail didn't open hers. "Merry Christmas."

"Merry Christmas." Charlie said, as he backed away from Susan's workstation. He turned back to his Aunt. "Well, I'd better get back to my office. Try as we might, the code doesn't write itself."

Abigail stepped forward, putting her index finger in the air at shoulder height. "Can I ask you something?"

Charlie leaned back in surprise for a moment before recovering and saying, "Sure, what is it?" He clasped his hands together for a moment before opening them up to welcome his aunt's question.

Abigail didn't quite touch his shoulder as they walked toward the door. "How do you do it?"

"Do what?"

"Christmas. The wreaths. The cards." She lifted the still-unopened one she had in her hand and gestured to Charlie with it. He stopped and turned to look at her, curious as to where his aunt was going with this. She stopped and looked at him before continuing, "I was there with you the night they died. Sometimes it feels like it happened yesterday. Doesn't-doesn't it bother you?"

Charlie closed his eyes for a moment. He wanted to hug his aunt. It had been so long since anyone talked about his parents and what happened. He took in a deep breath to compose himself. He didn't know how she'd react if he acted on his impulse. She might never speak to him again. He didn't want to jeopardize the progress they appeared to be making. He opened his eyes and saw the concern in his aunt's gaze. He smiled to show her that he was okay.

"I don't blame Christmas, Aunt Abigail. I don't believe that if it had been a different day, things would be different. Christmas didn't have anything to do with what happened to my parents."

"It's probably for the best that your mother's relatives were your guardians. I don't think you would have turned out this good if you'd been stuck with me."

Charlie leaned back, looking as though he was trying to process what Abigail had said. "Come on, now, Aunt Abigail." He straightened up and pulled the door open. "I don't think it would've been as bad as you think." He went to step out the door, but then twisted back around and grinned at her, pointing at the unopened Christmas card. "You better not give this away to anyone else. It has your name written on it." He winked at her before he shut the door.

"Ever the optimist."

Abigail told herself she had left the office at ten because she was catching up on the work she couldn't finish the night before. She also tried to convince herself that driving ten miles under the speed limit was due to her not wanting a repeat of the night before. It had nothing to do with thinking Jacob's ghost might be waiting for her once she got home to the Victorian country house he was in love with so much that he moved the business here ten years ago. Not that it seemed to matter where she was. The ghost had shown up at the office. The desk that used to belong to him at the office. Could he show up anywhere, anytime? What if he appeared in the passenger seat when she was driving? Which would be worse than having a cat run out in front of her car! Could he actually do that? Or was he only allowed to go where he'd spent most of his time? Had Jacob ever even been in her car before? Abigail tried to remember. She doubted it. This was her nice but practical car. Jacob's fancy car was in the garage. She had no qualms about sitting at his desk or living in his house- albeit sleeping in a room which was not the master bedroom- but she didn't need or want his car. What to do with it?

She had arrived at her driveway with no answers to her questions, relieved that the ride had been trouble-free. As soon as the headlights lit up the area around the house, Abigail saw a shape dart away, a fleeting glimpse of a small figure scurrying off into the darkness. *Is it that cat again!?!* She stepped out of the car and slammed the door shut behind her, the loud noise hopefully scaring off the feline intruder.

She trudged around her car to the front step. "You're not welcome here!" She shook her red-gloved fist in the air towards the direction she thought the cat had run off. She looked down at the snow around her front step. "Odd." No paw prints. There was, however, some boot prints in the snow. She looked back down her driveway. Yes, there was some tire tracks in the snow. She'd been so distracted by the prospect of the cat from the road reappearing she hadn't noticed them when she pulled in. The boot prints went to her front door and back to the driveway. "Curioser and curioser."

Abigail checked the mailbox. Empty. "Well, whoever it was didn't leave a note. Must not have been important," she muttered to herself while opening the door to get inside. After stripping off her coat, she changed out of her boots and into some slippers. She conducted a quick sweep of the house for any cats waiting in ambush. Once she was satisfied there were no cats lurking in the cupboards, Abigail put on the kettle to make herself some tea.

Having done that, she retrieved the Christmas card from Charlie, opened the envelope, walked over to the fireplace and turned the dial, the flames igniting with a satisfying crackle. While she looked at the card, the flames danced. Abigail turned the dial up another notch to get a good sized fire going. She stood the card up on the mantle. She turned around to find Jacob sitting in the chair again, his figure illuminated by the warm, flickering glow of the fire. The sight made her jump.

"Would you stop doing that?!?"

"What? I'm just sitting in a chair," Jacob said, all innocence. The spirit was becoming an infestation of the worst sort. Abigail strode past the chair on her way to the adjoining kitchen where she poured the hot water into a white mug with the word BOSS on it in bold red letters.

"At least I wasn't holding my drink this time." She dropped an infuser ball into the water, picked up the mug and went back over to the fireplace. Jacob continued just sitting there, looking at her.

"What?" she asked.

"Feeling a little neglected, are we?" He looked pointedly at the lone Christmas card on the fireplace mantle. "Is that what's got you so miffed?"

"No," Abigail walked over to the chair. "Maybe a little. Last year it was coping with your death and breaking off the engagement with what's his name. This year, you're both still gone. And, of the two of you, I never expected you'd be the one I'd be seeing again."

"A valid point."

Abigail sighed, looking down into her tea cup. The aroma of the hot chamomile tea wafted around them, a faint hint of honey and lemon floating on the steam. "I just got so used to being independent, I don't think I know how to connect with other people anymore."

"Sadly, that was never my strongest suit, either."

Abigail raised her eyes up from her tea. "Oh, come on! With your string of women?"

"That's something entirely different, as you well know. Besides, we both know they were far more interested in my money than me," Jacob said. A sly grin crept over his face. "Which is a pity, really. Because I was such a fascinating person once you got to know me." They shared a laugh at that. Abigail's eyes softened with fondness as she looked at Jacob.

"You were, really. I learned so much from you. And I do miss you, sometimes. Now, please, get out of my chair. I want to drink my tea in comfort and peace."

Understanding this, Jacob nodded and stood. His form melted away. Abigail sat down, the cold imprint of Jacob's specter sent a chill up her spine. It was gone just as quickly. She leaned back into the chair, her gaze landed on the card propped up on the mantle. The comforting warmth of the tea didn't relax her much. Despite her efforts, inner peace continued to elude her.

THE CAT OF

CHRISTMAS

PRESENT

Chapter Six

In the quiet of the one o'clock hour, the Cat of Christmas Present prowled across the floor, over to the overstuffed chair, where Abigail dozed, unaware. With a sudden and graceful pounce, it landed on her lap, startling her awake. She sprang up from the chair, causing its legs to screech on the floor as it skidded backward and sending the Siamese cat tumbling to the ground. An Indignant yowl resonated through the room. He shook himself, releasing an enchanting aroma that filled the air with the scents of fresh snow and evergreen needles, before he padded over to sit in front of the fireplace. His tail twitched in annoyance as he glared at Abigail.

"You!!" Abigail said, once she'd recovered from the abrupt awakening. She looked around, then back to the cat. "How did you get in here?"

The Cat of Christmas Present sat on the floor, illuminated by the soft glow of the fireplace, its bright blue eyes continued to glare at her. It was as if it was awaiting Abigail's next move.

"Well, what do you want?"

"Meow." *I'm the Cat of Christmas Present. I'm here to show you what's happening right in front of you.* The Siamese cat stood up and walked away from the fireplace. Abigail followed the cat, wondering where it was leading her. He stood at her front door, looked up at her and meowed. *Come on, we don't have all night.*

"It's freezing out there! I don't want to go out there." Abigail appealed to the cat. "Wouldn't it be better to stay here where it's nice and warm?"

At this, the Cat of Christmas Present sat down and looked back at the fireplace it had walked away from. He looked up at Abigail again. "Meow." *Well, we actually do have all night . . .*

Abigail, assuming the Siamese cat still insisted on going outside, opened the door. He remained seated, gazing up at her. "Look, if you want to go out there, go ahead," she said. "I'm not going to keep this open any longer." A few moments passed with neither of them moving. "Guess we're gonna stay here then." Abigail started to close the door.

The Cat of Christmas Present stood up and meowed. *We really should be going.*

"Oh, would you make up your mind already?!?" Abigail crouched down to pick the Siamese up. As she grabbed him, the air in front of her buzzed and light seemed to pour from his fur.

Abigail blinked as her eyes adjusted to the bright Christmas lights decorating Margot's Cocoa Cafe. She looked around for a clock because there is no way Margot would have the cafe open at one in the morning. Sure enough the clock displayed the time of ten to eight. "Hey!" she exclaimed as the Siamese jumped out of her arms and onto the counter four feet away with one graceful movement. "Aren't you the Cat of Christmas Present?" The cat turned his head to blink at her as if asking her 'whatever can you mean?'

Abigail pointed to the clock behind the cafe's owner. "This was yesterday, as in, the past."

The Siamese let out a yowl that should've made everyone in the cafe stop what they were doing and look at it, if they could've heard it. The Cat of Christmas Present sat down and glared at Abigail. *Once again, you are missing the point. Christmas Present isn't just today or tomorrow or the day after that. You are so focused on being right you can't see beyond your narrow definition of how things should be.*

The Siamese shook his head, stood up and sauntered across the counter. He got to one of the white ceramic sugar packet holders and daintily plucked a single packet out with his teeth. He dropped it on the counter and began to bat it across the surface, past the oblivious customers. Abigail watched the cat's antics, amused, in spite of herself. She walked down to where the cat was pouncing on the packet, wondering if anyone could see this sugar packet moving across the counter, and if they did, if they're thinking, "Maybe I should lay off the sugar and caffeine for a bit."

The Cat of Christmas Present batted the sugar packet into the mug of one of the customers. It was Charlie. He was chatting with a black haired young man who Abigail recognized. She couldn't recall his name, but he appeared to be friends with Charlie.

"No surprise there," Abigail crossed her arms and leaned against the counter for a better view of their conversation. The Cat of Christmas Present chirped at her inquisitively.

"He's so open and friendly, everyone likes him."

The Siamese chirped again and purred in agreement.

"Yes, even me." Abigail continued. "But don't tell *him* that, it'll ruin my reputation."

The Cat of Christmas Past shook his head at Abigail's remark before turning to bat the sugar packet once more, only to find that Charlie was holding it up in his left hand, while he leaned on the counter. Charlie was wearing a sweater with a playful snowman design.

"Where'd this come from?" Charlie glanced over toward his buddy Benji, who was wearing a Santa hat.

"No clue." Benji shrugged his shoulders and raised his mug of hot chocolate with a cheerful "Merry Christmas!"

"Merry Christmas!" Charlie flipped the packet back up the counter (the Siamese in hot pursuit) and grabbed his own mug of hot chocolate. Clinking his mug against Benji's, they took a sip, their drinks now infused with holiday cheer.

"You don't know what you're missing," said Benji. "You should come up to the cabin with the rest of us. You're practically the only one who's not going to be there." When Charlie's only response was to drink more of his hot chocolate, Benji continued. "It's not too late. AppDevPlus booked a spot for you anyway. I'm sure one of us can find room in the SUV to squeeze you in."

"Squeeze me in?"

"Yeah."

Charlie laughed and shook his head. "No thanks. The Great Outdoors has never been my thing. I like being right here, in civilization."

"Right, because Little Dickens is a major metropolis." Benji rolled his eyes.

"It's still got more than a cabin."

"I beg to differ. This cabin has all the amenities. We won't need a town."

"If you say so." The corner of Charlie's mouth quirked up.

"Anyway, you never said, did she like the wreath?" Benji asked, changing the subject abruptly.

"My Aunt? No," Charlie chuckled, a rueful smile on his face. "She gave it away to charity."

"No, man. Not your Aunt--Susan." Benji corrected him, nudging Charlie with his elbow. The nudge caused Charlie to slosh hot chocolate onto the counter, creating a chocolatey splash that resembled a reindeer's antler.

"Hey!" Charlie stood up from the stool he was sitting on to move away from Benji and grab some napkins. Benji simply shrugged and mouthed 'Whoops', his grin showing how not sorry he was. Charlie wiped up the puddle of hot chocolate on the wooden counter. "She never said. But I think she must like it."

"How do you figure that?"

Charlie sat back down on the stool and set down his mug. "Because," he turned to face Benji. "I saw it was hanging on her front door when I drove by her house."

Benji laughed and nudged Charlie again. "Stalker much? You are hopeless!"

"No, you and Lily are hopeless. I'm glad I'm not going to be there to witness the two of you continue your dance of avoidance in an exotic new setting."

Benji recoiled dramatically at Charlie's words. Exaggerating the effect they had on him, pretending to balance precariously on the edge of the stool. He gripped the counter with one hand while clutching at his heart with the other. The french doors of the cafe open, the bells jingle to announce the entrance of a group of five fellow employees of AppDevPlus. One of which was the aforementioned Lily. She saw Charlie and waved at him, her black pig-tails swinging like Christmas bells.

Charlie waved back. "Speak of the devil. . ." He jutted his chin toward the cafe doors where the group was standing. The other four noticed Lily waving and followed her gaze to see Charlie sitting with Benji. Benji spun his stool around to wave at the group and smile at Lily, his Santa hat illuminated, at the press of a button, with a string of tiny twinkling LED lights. Then he spun back to drain the last of the hot chocolate from his mug.

He plunked the empty mug down on the counter. "For that remark, this one's on you." Benji scooped his coat and gym bag from the floor. "I'm out of here. Merry Christmas, Charlie."

"Merry Christmas, Benji." Charlie waved goodbye to Benji and the other AppDevPlus employees as they left the cafe, the sound of their laughter cut off by the closing of the door.

Charlie turned back to his mug of hot chocolate and looked at the contents as if they held the answer to some great mystery, if he could only gaze at it long enough.

"It's not going to stop getting colder the longer you stare at it," Margot said, standing a few feet away, washing the mugs and glasses in the sink behind the counter. "Not unless you've got heat-ray vision like one of those super-heroes."

The comment made Charlie laugh. "No, that I do not. But it certainly would be handy this time of year."

"Sure would," Margot said and started drying the mugs and glasses with a tea towel with a smiling yeti wearing a scarf design on it.

Charlie looked up at the clock. Abigail followed his gaze and saw the clock now read five after eight. When she looked back at Charlie, he was looking into his mug again. The Cat of Christmas Present sat between Abigail and Charlie.

"Meow." *You were still in town, working at the office.*

"Don't look at me like that. This isn't my fault. He had other options. It was his choice to be sitting here, staring into his hot chocolate. It's probably not even me he's thinking about. He's twenty-three, he's probably thinking about driving by Susan's house again."

The Cat of Christmas Present put his ears back and let out a hiss which sounded like someone dropping a chain of sleigh bells on the floor.

"He should have asked her. She probably would have said yes and she'd be sitting there having a better time than whatever it is she's doing right now. I mean, then. Whenever!"

The Cat of Christmas Present's ears perked up. Abigail looked at Charlie sitting a few feet away from her, oblivious to her presence. She normally didn't look at him for very long. It made her feel uncomfortable, now she understood why.

"Why did he have to come here? There are plenty of companies looking for programmers. Until he moved here, I hadn't seen him since he was a child. It had been years. When he showed up out of the blue, it was such a shock." Abigail walked closer to where Charlie was sitting. "Seeing him was . . . it was like seeing . . ."

"Meow?" *A ghost?*

"He looks so much like his father . . ." Abigail reached out to put her hand on Charlie's shoulder.

The Cat of Christmas Present leapt forward and, as her fingers grazed its fur, a bright light glowed from the cat's body, filling the cafe with radiance.

Ethan Clarke sat in solitude at a small table in Margot's Cocoa Cafe, his eyes occasionally drifting from his phone to the window where snowflakes danced in the night. The blue light of his phone cast a thoughtful shadow across his features, highlighting a furrow of concentration as he read his boss's last message: 'Persistence, Ethan. Keep at it. Make it happen.' Followed by dollar sign emojis. His fingers absentmindedly traced the rim of his half-empty hot chocolate mug, lost in thought.

Margot noticed Ethan in his quiet contemplation and approached with a warm, inviting smile.

"Can I get you a refill, or maybe a strong espresso to shake off the chill?" she asked, her voice echoing the warmth of the cafe.

Ethan's eyes lifted, and a small, grateful smile appeared. "The hot chocolate is perfect, thank you. It's like a warm blanket on a night like this."

Margot's gaze briefly flicked to the phone on the table before meeting Ethan's eyes again.

"Tough night, huh? Girlfriend giving you a hard time for being away on Christmas Eve?" she asked, a playful chuckle in her voice.

He responded with a gentle shake of his head, his smile still lingering. "Oh, no, I don't have a girlfriend. It's just... work stuff," A hint of defensiveness crept into his tone.

Margot raised an eyebrow, her voice soft yet teasing. "Work on Christmas Eve? Must be important. Or is it one of those 'saving the world' jobs?"

"Hardly saving the world," Ethan replied, trying to keep the conversation light. "Just trying to... make a deal happen."

Pouring him a fresh mug of hot chocolate, Margot studied him for a moment with a mix of curiosity and empathy. "Well, sometimes the best deals are the ones you don't make. Especially if they keep you from enjoying Christmas," she advised.

His smile grew warmer, reflecting a sense of ease that wasn't there before. "Is that the voice of experience, or just the holiday spirit?"

"A little of both. Enjoy your hot chocolate. On the house. Merry Christmas."

As Margot moved away, Ethan watched her with a newfound appreciation, the warmth from the hot chocolate mirroring the warmth he felt inside. The pressures of work felt a little lighter, eased by the unexpected but welcome exchange.

Chapter Seven

A bigail found herself standing in the cramped hallway of a strange house. The walls were a dull gray and the wooden floors had deep scratches from years of wear and tear. She looked down at the Siamese cat at her feet. The cat's tail twitched as it waited for her next move.

"Where are we? Who do I know that would live here?"

"Meow." *Follow me and you'll find out.* The Cat of Christmas Present, tail in the air, padded quietly down the hall and turned into the first doorway on the right. Abigail shrugged to herself. She didn't have much choice but to follow the cat down the hall. When she entered the room through the doorway on the right she was greeted with the sight of her architect, Susan, standing on the second rung from the top of a step ladder. The sight stopped her in her tracks. Susan had her long black hair tucked into a messy bun with a reindeer antler headband on her head. She was wearing a very ugly Christmas sweater over green yoga pants with yellow presents with red bows all over them. Even though she knew Susan couldn't see or hear her, Abigail covered her mouth to stifle a laugh. She knew Susan would be mortified if she knew her boss had seen her looking like this.

Once she recovered from seeing her architect in her festive casual attire, Abigail noticed that there was someone holding the ladder Susan was standing on. It was a man. He had short, black hair. The hand he was holding the ladder with was steady. His arms looked strong. He was sitting in a wheelchair. Abigail wondered who this man was. Susan had never mentioned a boyfriend. Abigail didn't encourage much conversation outside of business. As Abigail was working this out in her head, the man spoke.

"Have you ever considered how much work this is, only to have to take it back down in a week?" His brown eyes held a mischievous glint as Susan struggled to untangle a strand of gold garland.

"It wouldn't be a week if you let me get a tree sooner."

"And have it drop needles all month long? No thanks."

"You know, you and Abigail have a lot in common. I bet you'd get along if you'd ever let me tell people about you."

"Did Abigail help you decorate the tree in the office?"

"I said a lot, not everything. I just think that you two would hit it off if you ever met."

"I hear you complain about your boss all the time and this is the person you want to set me, your beloved and only brother, up with? Wait, no. That actually makes total sense."

Susan dropped the strand of garland onto her brother's head.

"I do not complain about my boss all the time, *Timothy*. And I might consider setting you up with someone to get you out of my hair, but I could never inflict my brother on my boss."

"You do realize that I'm holding this ladder for you, don't you?"

"You wouldn't dare."

"I might if you call me Timothy again. You know I hate that."

"Fine. Fine, Tim."

"Better. But I wouldn't because that would be two of us rolling around in a wheelchair, wouldn't it? And this place is already cramped enough with one wheelchair and a Christmas tree."

Susan went down a few rungs so she could grab the garland off of Tim's head.

"Ouch! Hey, watch it. That's some of my hair you got there."

"Sorry," Susan went back up the ladder, snickering as she did.

"Yeah, you sound it."

This made Susan burst out laughing. She started putting the garland around the tree.

"Listen . . . I'll ask Abigail about getting some time off to help you with your recovery in the new year. I can't ask now. It's not a good time to ask now."

"With your boss, it's never a good time to ask. You probably would've had better luck with the old boss. Just my luck to get an injury that no one can figure out."

"And such a freak injury, too. Every doctor you've gone to has diagnosed it as something different." said Susan, ignoring the remark about her boss. She was off the ladder and digging into a brown box of ornaments.

Tim let go of the ladder to take the brakes off his wheelchair and turn it to join his sister and poke through the ornaments.

"All I know for sure is that I can't put any weight on my legs." He shrugged.

Both Susan and Tim had their backs to the tree. They couldn't see the branches moving, but Abigail could. The Cat of Christmas Present poked his head out from some branches in the middle of the tree.

"What are you doing?!?" Abigail hissed at the cat, looking from the siblings to the tree. She edged around the coffee table and ladder to get closer to the cat and the wobbling tree.

"We'll find the right doctor and figure out what needs to happen to get you on the road to recovery," Susan put her arm around Tim's shoulders and gave a short squeeze.

Abigail reached up and steadied the tree. She scowled down at the Siamese cat. "Are you trying to kill them by knocking this tree down on top of them?!?"

The Cat of Christmas Present looked up at Abigail through the branches. He let out an innocent mew. *Of course not!*

"Don't give me that. I know you. You have a penchant for mayhem, cat!" She grabbed at the Siamese, disappearing into the branches of the tree herself. As she and the cat were surrounded by a flash of light, Abigail could faintly hear Tim's words.

"Wouldn't that be a Christmas miracle?"

The Cat of Christmas Present scampered down the dimly lit hall away from Abigail. Abigail has never set foot in this building before, either. But she knew immediately where they were.

"What are we doing at the hospital the night before Christmas Eve? Did something happen to Charlie? Susan? Susan's Brother?"

"Meow." The Cat of Christmas Present danced in the hall with excitement. *Come see! Come see!*

Abigail followed the Siamese cat and soon found herself standing at the threshold of the Children's Ward. It was quiet except for the faint hums and occasional, rhythmic beeps from some of the machines beside the beds. Eight children lay in their beds-- four on each side. The Siamese cat began to purr, filling the room with its rumbling sound.

One of the children stirred and whispered: "I hear purring."

"Me too!" another child whispered back.

"It can't be. It's the middle of the night," whispered another. One of the children had sat up at this point. To Abigail's surprise, the children not only heard the purring but could also see the cat.

"It is a cat!" The child sat up and slid out of the bed and approached the Siamese cat, which sat in the middle of the room. The other two children able to get out of their beds soon joined the first child in petting the Cat of Christmas Present. The children that were hooked up to equipment used their remotes to raise the head of their beds so they too could see the cat.

"How did it get in here?"

"What kind of cat is it?"

"It's so pretty!"

Its whiskers shimmered with the sweet, comforting scent of freshly baked gingerbread cookies.

"Its fur is so soft."

His soft, silky fur carried the subtle fragrance of freshly fallen snow.

"Can I see?" said the child in the first bed. The first child out of bed picked up the Cat of Christmas Present, and as one, the three children carried it over to the child in the first bed. The gentle purring of the cat was like a melodic invitation, conjuring images of warm, crackling fireplaces and cozy gatherings, filled with the rich aroma of cinnamon and nutmeg. Then, with tenderness, they moved the cat to the next bed so that child could also experience the solace of its presence.

The child in the first bed now watched as the cat brought joy to the other children. Abigail stood by, amazed by the power of this simple visit.

"Are you an angel?"

The question startled Abigail. She hadn't imagined that the children could see her, too. They were all paying attention to the cat, not her.

Abigail shook her head. "No."

"Then how did you and the cat get inside after visiting hours?"

Abigail stepped closer. "Well, really, the cat brought me to the hospital."
"Why?"

Abigail smiled, her heart touched by the innocence before her. "To see you."

Abigail woke up with a smile on her face. How long had it been since that happened? Quite some time. Maybe after Wallace had proposed to her. The image of the child at the hospital smiling back at her came back to her. She sat up and perched on the side of her bed. She remembered seeing all of the children there in the hospital. They weren't going home for the holidays. They'd be spending Christmas in the hospital.

She recalled the wonder in their little whispers as they heard the purring. Abigail remembered the delight on their little faces when they saw the cat in the middle of the room. The cat made them happy. Smoky had made her happy. To her parents, it had seemed like such an insignificant thing that she'd quickly forget about. And she had, but it hadn't made what happened any less of a betrayal or less painful. Those feelings were still with her, all these years later. Why else would they have shown up? It meant the world to a child.

Abigail walked over to her dresser to get ready for work. She looked in the mirror at her reflection.

"I've been so blind."

Abigail wasn't shocked to find the flier she threw in the garbage was now magically sitting on her desk when she got in the office that morning.

"Perfect." she said, as she sat down. She pulled out the checkbook from the top drawer. She pulled up the accounting program on her laptop. She grabbed her pen and wrote the Little Dickens Hospital a check matching the amount the past gala raised. In the check memo, after consulting the flier, she wrote "Feline Fine and Canine Cuddles" program.

Abigail heard the door to the office open. She looked up to see Susan entering, wearing a festive red and green scarf.

"Great, you're here! Once you've got your coat off, meet me over at the drafting table."

"Yes, Ms. Carson," Susan was surprised to see Abigail sitting at her desk already. When she got to the drafting table, she found Abigail waiting for her with the plans for the new community center out.

"Wait a minute, Ms. Carson," Susan said. "Those are the old plans for the center."

"Yes, they are," Abigail replied. "They are so much more accessible than the new plans, aren't they?"

Susan looked down for a moment, feeling called out. Then she straightened up.

"Yes, they were."

"Why did you let me take them out? Why didn't you state how important they are for a community building?"

"You were adamant that there was enough and," Susan decided to lay it all on the line. "I didn't want to lose the most important features by trying to get them all approved."

"Huh. Well, I guess I'm just like most people in the world. I don't think about accessibility until life makes me think about it."

"Until a year and a half ago, I didn't think about it much myself."

"What changed a year and a half ago?"

"My brother was hurt in a sporting accident. He's had multiple conflicting assessments, he might need surgery but because his condition doesn't appear to be life-threatening he keeps getting shuffled around from specialist to specialist. We thought he'd be back up and walking by now. I'm sorry. I'm babbling. I never meant to burden you with my problems."

"Susan," Abigail looked at her architect from across the drafting table. "Are you telling me that your brother's been here for a year and a half? And you haven't mentioned this to me? Why?"

"I-how?" Susan gasped and looked at her boss with her mouth hanging open in surprise for a moment. She closed her mouth and took a breath to collect herself. "Sorry, but how did you know my brother was here? He's extremely proud and embarrassed that he needs a wheelchair to get around. He didn't want anyone to know. And you were always so busy and then Jacob died around this time last year and there just never seemed to be a good time to bring it up."

"I-I just assumed that he was here. Sorry to give you the impression you somehow let it slip that he was here." Abigail didn't want to have to try and explain exactly how she found out about Susan's brother.

"So, now you know." Susan said, looking relieved she was no longer the only one that knew her brother was here without having betrayed the secret.

"Now I know," Abigail nodded. "So, now that we've talked about going back to these more accessible plans for the community center, why don't you take the rest of the day off."

"Really? The rest of the day off?" Susan could hardly believe her ears. "A-are you sure?"

"Of course, I'm sure. The town's planning department doesn't open again until next year, so there's no rush to get the revisions to them. Go home. Spend the rest of the day with your family."

"Thank you, Ms. Carson!" Susan said and got her coat and purse to head home. "Aren't you heading home, too?" She asked when she saw Abigail was back at her desk.

Abigail nodded. "I have a few things to take care of before I do."

"Merry Christmas, Ms. Carson!" Susan left the office before her boss had the opportunity to change her mind.

Abigail got her coat and purse. When she returned to her desk she found Jacob sitting in her chair again. He had his feet up on the desk like he used to. He smiled at her and held out the flier and check out for her.

"Don't forget these."

"Thank you." Abigail plucked them from his hands and closed up the office.

Abigail headed straight for the reception desk at the Little Dickens Hospital to ask about the doctors who had been canvassing for donations.

"Excuse me!" She called and waved to the woman behind the glass partition.

On the way, Abigail spotted the wreath Charlie gave her on one of the doors just down the hall. She stopped mid-wave. "Nevermind." She folded her fingers into a fist as she changed direction to knock on the door.

"Come in!" a voice called from inside. Dr. Ifhram was sitting at a desk cluttered with papers and a small Christmas tree adorned with twinkling lights and ornaments. It was clear that she was doing some last minute number crunching for the animal-assisted therapy campaign.

"Sorry to bother you on Christmas Eve. I've got more work for you, I'm afraid." Abigail stepped forward and held out the check to her.

Dr. Ifhram started at the sound of Abigail's voice. She stared disbelieving at the check Abigail was holding out to her. She took it with some hesitation. "Ms. Carson. This is most generous!" She said, looking at the check. She looked up at Abigail, her eyes shining with gratitude. "What made you change your mind?"

"Christmas."

"Merry Christmas, Ms. Carson!" Dr. Ifhram wished her with a heartfelt smile. The room seemed to glow with the magic of the season.

Abigail smiled and nodded at the doctor. She left the hospital, stepping out into the crisp winter air. She let out a sigh of relief, her breath forming little puffs of fog in the chilly air. She did it. It hadn't been the easiest thing to do. But, it hadn't been as difficult as she thought it might have been. Abigail got into her car feeling better about herself.

Abigail moved about her big, empty house. She watched as the last of the light faded from the sky. The tea in her mug had grown cold and she swirled it around, lost in thought. Once darkness fell, Abigail found herself humming random bits of Christmas carols to herself as she walked around - "Hark! The Herald Angels Sing" and "Joy to the World." She couldn't help noticing how bare her undecorated living space was. It looked so sad and drab compared to Susan's place and the office - also thanks to Susan. She found herself drawn to the Christmas card sitting on top of her fireplace mantle.

"What are you so pleased about?" Jacob's voice sliced through her thoughts like the crisp winter wind. The sound made Abigail turn around; he was sitting in her chair again.

"What do you mean?" Abigail set down her mug, placing it back on its saucer on an exquisitely carved coffee table.

"You're strutting around here, thinking you've done a good deed, aren't you?"

"Well, haven't I? That gift will make a difference. I see that now, with help from the cat."

"Yes, yes, yes." Jacob waved his hand loosely in agreement. "It will make a difference in the lives of those children. That is all well and good." He stood up and began circling around Abigail. "But will it make a difference in your life?" Jacob pointed his finger at her.

"What? Of course it will."

"Besides the tax write off."

"It. Will." Abigail glared at Jacob.

"Will it, really?" Jacob stopped walking and stood behind her. "You think a large donation and putting back the accessibility features you should never have taken out in the first place is going to make a lasting difference in the path you are headed down?'

"One step at a time, Jacob. One step at a time." Abigail looked over her shoulder at Jacob, only to find that he was gone, leaving behind a faint scent of ozone. She huffed in annoyance, then went up to bed.

THE CAT OF

CHRISTMAS

FUTURE

Chapter Eight

A bigail lay in bed, her eyes closed. She was starting to drift off to sleep when she felt a sudden urge to turn over. She opened her eyes and gasped. Sitting on her bedside table was an enormous cat. The lights were on. Abigail was certain she had turned off all the lights before crawling into bed.

The cat radiated a mysterious and enchanting aroma that wove the future and the past into the present moment. Its thick, dark fur, a cloak of shadows and secrets, held the deep, comforting scent of the wild forests of its lineage, reminiscent of ancient tales and hidden paths through snow-laden trees.

She propped herself up on her left elbow, not taking her eyes off the giant feline. It regarded her with an intent, unblinking stare. Abigail knew this was not an ordinary cat - it had to be the Cat of Christmas Future, here to show her glimpses of what was to come.

The Cat of Christmas Future didn't meow as the other two cats had. It simply stared at Abigail. She cleared her throat, unnerved.

"You must be the Cat of Christmas Future." The cat did nothing in response. "That's not creepy at all." She said to the cat.

The Cat of Christmas Future leaped down from the bedside table and glided across the room over to the window. Subtler notes lingered in its wake; a complex tapestry of the natural world, the mystique of the unknown, and the timeless spirit of the Yuletide season. Abigail watched as the window, which had been closed and locked only moments before, opened, seemingly of its own accord, letting in the chilly winter breeze.

"I know, I know," Abigail threw off her covers with a sigh of resignation. "I went through this with the Cat of Christmas Past. Let's cut out the chase scene and get right to the point. I've learned a lot from my time with the other two cats. I'm looking forward to what you have to show me now." She reached out with both hands to pick it up, the light coming from the cat intensifying as she made contact. There was a flash of light that filled the room and Abigail felt a surge of energy as she held the giant cat in her arms.

When the blinding light subsided, Abigail blinked in shock at the grim scene before her. She shook her head and blinked again before looking back to see the scene unchanged: a room full of white walls, glass windows, and a wheelchair-bound figure in the middle. Susan's brother, Tim, was seated in the wheelchair, motionless and expressionless. He stared out one of the windows, unable to see past his own reflection in the glass. There was a feeling of emptiness in the room that left the space with an almost tangible sadness.

"What's going on here?" Abigail turned to the cat. "I thought that Tim was going to get better. What is he doing here?"

The Cat of Christmas Future sat and turned its head to look at the door. Abigail followed the cat's gaze and saw Susan enter the visiting room with a doctor she didn't recognize.

"I'm sorry, there's been no noticeable improvement. We did tell you both that due to the time between the occurrence of the injury and the surgery, the chances of success were lower. I wish that he had come to us sooner. There might have been a better chance of recovery."

"Might?" Susan raised an eyebrow at the doctor and crossed her arms over her chest, her sweater featuring a pattern of reindeer and snowflakes.

"Would." The doctor's eyes met Susan's for an instant before he looked away.

"How much sooner?" Susan uncrossed her arms to angle them outwards, her hands palm up to the ceiling.

"It's hard to know with the damage that we couldn't see from the scans. But, even six months would've helped."

"I wish we'd known that a year ago. Maybe then, his surgery wouldn't have been bumped back again." Susan dropped her hands to her sides. Her shoulders slumped in defeat.

"I'm sorry that we didn't know the extent of your brother's injury until we opened him up."

"No, this is all my fault." Susan shook her head. Now she was the one not looking at the doctor. "I'm the one who kept saying I needed more time to get the project done. Once it was done, then I'd have time to help him with his recovery. I'm the reason we waited so long. And it was all for nothing."

Abigail watched Susan walk away from the doctor, over to the window on the other side of the room, where a Christmas tree stood decorated with ornaments and twinkling lights.. It was clear from her words that Susan blamed herself for what happened to her brother. Now they were standing there in the same room. Together, but worlds apart. Tears streamed down her cheeks as she looked over at Tim and realized the truth of her brother's situation. Abigail was torn between who she wanted to comfort first. Tim, because of how everything had gone so wrong. Or Susan, because, even though Tim wasn't able to have the surgery, she still had her brother. Or did she? Abigail felt a lump form in her throat as she watched Susan try to keep it together for Tim's sake. She knew how hard it must be for Susan to stay strong while facing this heartbreaking reality.

Abigail took another look at Tim sitting at the window. It was as if he was a statue, oblivious to the fact his sister and the doctor were in the room. She watched as the doctor exited the room with long, silent steps. Then she turned to the Cat of Christmas Future.

"Let's go."

The hospital visiting room was filled with a blinding light.

The Cat of Christmas Future transported them into the middle of a room in disarray. Half of it was empty, the other half contained two boxes piled in a haphazard manner. Abigail looked around in disbelief. This was *her* house.

"My house! What's happened to it? Where is all my furniture? Where are all my books?!" Abigail asked, her voice tinged with confusion and concern as she took in the emptiness that had taken over her home.

The Cat of Christmas Future turned its unblinking eyes to the front door. The jingling of keys could be heard as someone opened the door. Abigail's nephew, Charlie entered, followed by Benji, the co-worker she saw him sitting with at Margot's Cocoa Cafe.

"Shut the door?" Benji stopped and grabbed the door.

"Leave it open," Charlie shook his head. "We aren't staying long. There are only two boxes left." The two young men walked over to the boxes on the floor.

"Man, I know she didn't like Christmas." Benji said, glancing around at the bare walls. "But did she have to ruin it for everyone else?"

"Not *everyone* else."

"There are a lot of people lining up for unemployment thanks to the community center project folding now that McBane Properties acquired Morris and Carson Development." Benji stopped and shivered on the spot.

"Are you okay?" Charlie said slowly, as he took a step back from his friend. "You look like someone just walked over your grave."

"I was just thinking. They are both dead, in the span of three years." Benji gave Charlie a side-long look. "What if – what if the business is cursed?"

"What?!?" Charlie felt the blood drain from his face at this question. "The company was here for ten years before Jacob died. How is that being cursed?"

"I don't know, maybe because your aunt also just died?" Benji shrugged.

"And you think she planned it? I doubt Jacob planned on dying when he did. My aunt fought off the takeover attempts of McBane Properties to the end. She pretty much died trying to get that community center project off the ground."

"You're still sticking up for her. Even though you're the one that got stuck with handling her estate. She never appreciated you. I guess I'll never understand it."

"You're right. She didn't appreciate me. She didn't know me. I didn't know her. And that's why I can do this for her, now. She wouldn't let anyone in while she was alive. At least, now that she's gone, she's letting someone help her."

"Well, she's dead. It's not like she has much choice."

"Neither did Susan. She had too much on her plate to keep the company going. With her brother's medical bills piling up, the only thing she could do was sell." Charlie's head hung low as he kicked the wooden flooring with the toe of his boot.

"I'm sorry it didn't work out with you and Susan." Benji placed a comforting hand on Charlie's shoulder.

A wry grin twisted Charlie's lips upward. "Hey, I've still got you, don't I?" He raised his head up, eyes glinting with mischief. "And now, you can help me, by getting that box over there." Charlie gestured towards the corner of the room.

Charlie grabbed the top box, feeling the weight of the cardboard in his hands. It was taped shut. A piece of paper with neat handwriting that read "Abigail's Estate" was taped on the side.

"I'm dead?" Abigail said in disbelief.

Benji crouched down, his arms flexing against the weight of the box. It was heavier than he thought. He adjusted his grip, one arm around the bottom and the other at the side. He rose to his full height and tried to steady himself. "What's in this?" he groaned and staggered toward the door.

"I'm dead." Abigail said it again. She shook her head. She didn't believe it.

"Books." Charlie's box was full of books, too.

Abigail watched as Benji and Charlie disappeared out the door, the weight of their boxes causing them to stagger. When they were gone, she turned her head and looked down at the Cat of Christmas Future.

"What happened to me?" The large, Norwegian Forest Cat stared back up at her.

Abigail swooped the cat up in one quick motion. She held it out at eye level, hands under its front legs. she scowled at it, searching for answers in its enigmatic gaze.

"What happened to me?!" Abigail demanded. There was a flash of bright light that seemed to come from the cat itself.

Abigail's hands were empty, the Cat of Christmas Future had vanished. A gust of bitter, sharp and unyielding wind whipped wet snowflakes in her face, taking her breath away. She turned around, only to find herself standing in front of a cluster of tombstones. These cold, unfeeling slabs of stone created a boundary between the living and the dead. The cemetery stretched out before her in a long, silent aisle of white which had no end.

As she wove her way through the thick fog that billowed around her feet, she caught sight of Cat of Christmas Future sitting on top of a tombstone. She made her way over to where the cat was sitting. It felt like her heart stopped when she saw her name chiseled into the tombsone.

"I don't believe this. I am perfectly healthy. I drink those green smoothies every day. This can't be the future!" Abigail turned away from the sight of her grave. It might not be a surprise, it was disturbing, nonetheless.

"It's called working yourself into an early grave, my dear."

"Jacob!" Abigail whirled around at the sound of his voice. Jacob stood behind the tombstone. The Cat of Christmas Future was as still as if it was made of stone, too. "It's not fair!"

"I don't recall anyone ever saying it was."

"I'm already changing. You saw that."

"Oh, yes. A big fat check and a few revisions to the community center and everything's supposed to be all better, is it?"

"Please," Abigail looked at the Cat of Christmas Future, then at Jacob. "Please, I can do better."

Jacob heaved a sigh. His shoulders slumped. He glanced down at the Cat of Christmas Future and shook his head. The Cat of Christmas Future looked up at Jacob.

"No, Abigail," said Jacob. "You can't."

"What?!?" Abigail was too surprised to say anything more. She stepped back, her mind reeling with confusion. Jacob sauntered from behind the tombstone and placed his hands on her shoulders. She felt the icy chill from his ethereal shade seep through her clothing.

"You've been doing better for quite some time--before I even entered your life. And where has it gotten you?"

"Apparently, it's gotten me to an early grave with a cat that can't meow and my mentor's ghost," Abigail answered acidly.

"If doing better was all that you needed, you'd already be there." Jacob let go of Abigail's shoulders and returned to stand next to the Cat of Christmas Future. "The Cats of Christmas Past, Present, and Future and I can only take you to the water. If you'll excuse the idiom. We can't make you drink it. You're the only one that can truly give yourself this chance. And only if you think you deserve it. For what it's worth, the cats and I think you are."

Jacob smiled at her before fading away completely. Abigail was too pre-occupied with absorbing everything he said to react before he completely faded.

The Cat of Christmas Future blinked at Abigail for the first time since she met him. She stretched out a hand to pet him. "Thank you."

CHRISTMAS DAY

Chapter Nine

The bright burst of light from the Cat of Christmas Future faded, and Abigail was transported back to her bedroom. She threw back the covers and jumped out of bed. She raced downstairs. Once at the bottom, Abigail scanned her surroundings. Everything was just as it had been when she went to bed. She ran over to the bookshelves. All her books were still on the shelves. She'd never been so happy to see them. She looked around the room. Her gaze landed on the lone Christmas card on the fireplace mantle. A flood of joy washed over her at the sight of it.

"Yesterday was a good start," she thought to herself. "But Jacob was right, it's time to make some lasting lifestyle changes."

As Abigail pulled open the door of Margot's Cocoa Café, bundled up in her winter coat and scarf, the bell chimed a merry greeting. She noticed that even in the cold, some customers had decided to brave the elements and were sitting inside, warming up with hot cocoa. She made her way to the counter where the proprietor was stood by the cash register.

"Margot, I wasn't sure if you'd be open . . . with it being Christmas and all."

"You aren't the only one in this town that doesn't take Christmas off, Abigail Carson. Besides, if we were closed, there'd be a riot. Can't be upsetting the routine of our devoted regulars, now can we?" Margot, wearing a Santa hat, nodded towards of a table full of seniors all huddled together, their laughter ringing through the café as they discussed the events of the morning over their steaming mugs. Abigail couldn't help but smile at the cozy scene and she turned back to Margot.

"Two hot cocoas, please. To go."

Margot gave Abigail the side-eye as she prepared her order. Abigail's smile drained away. She didn't understand why her ordering hot cocoa would merit such a response.

"You don't have Susan coming in to work with you this morning, do you?"

Abigail's expression changed from confusion to relief. Now, the strange look made sense.

"Absolutely not! I'm visiting my nephew, Charlie." She glanced around the cafe. Everyone seemed to be absorbed in their own Christmas business. Still, she lowered her voice as she continued. "Would you believe, I don't even have his number in my phone?!?" Margot nodded her head and gave Abigail a knowing smirk.

Abigail looked away from the smirk. *I guess I earned that,* she thought. Out loud, she said, "I really have done a fantasic job at keeping him at a distance. I don't understand why he never gave up on me."

With a begrudging grunt, Margot slid the tray of steaming hot cocoas across the counter to Abigail.

"In that case, they're on the house. Merry Christmas."

"Thank you." Abigail blinked, taken by surprise again. She picked up the tray. "Merry Christmas to you."

"And tell Charlie I wish him a Merry Christmas."

"I will," Abigail said and pushed open the door, almost knocking over Ethan Clarke. He stepped back and held the door open for her.

"You seem in good spirits today, Ms. Carson." He couldn't help but comment.

She looked up, a hint of surprise in her eyes. "It's Christmas, after all. A time for a little joy, don't you think?"

Ethan nodded. "Absolutely. And, for the record, I won't bring up anything about Morris and Carson or McBane Properties today. It's a day off from all that."

Abigail paused for a moment, assessing him. "You know, Ethan, if you're still around in the new year, maybe we could talk about a job. Something different from what you're used to, perhaps."

Ethan was taken aback by the offer. "I might just take you up on that, Ms. Carson. Thank you."

With a nod and a final smile, Abigail made her way to her car, leaving Ethan to contemplate the unexpected turn his Christmas morning had taken. He entered the cafe, the warmth enveloping him, now with a new perspective on what his future in Little Dickens might hold.

Behind the counter stood the woman who had served him the night before.

"Merry Christmas! Back for more hot chocolate?" she asked, her voice carrying the same warmth he remembered.

"Merry Christmas!" Ethan replied, "Coffee would be great, and whatever you recommend for breakfast."

"Of course. How about our Christmas special? Cinnamon rolls, fresh from the oven, and a side of fruit salad."

"That sounds great, thank you," Ethan took a seat by the window, the same spot as last night. He watched the gentle dance of snowflakes outside, the peaceful scene was a stark contrast to his usual hectic mornings.

Margot brought over his coffee and breakfast, placing them before him with a gentle smile. "Here you go. I hope you enjoy it. Let me know if you need anything else."

"Thank you. I didn't catch your name last night."

"Christmas Eve is a surprisingly busy night here. I'm Margot, the owner. And you are?"

"Ethan. Thanks for remembering me."

"It's not every day we get new faces around here, especially on Christmas," Margot flashed another smile at the young man before returning to the counter.

Ethan took a sip of the hot coffee, feeling the warmth spread through him. The cinnamon roll was soft and sweet, a perfect treat for Christmas morning. The stress and urgency that had been his constant companions for as long as he could remember began to fade, replaced by something new and unfamiliar. It was a bit unsettling, but he thought he liked it.

As Abigail walked through the snow-lined streets of Little Dickens, her gaze fell upon 'Thurston's Toy Shop.' It was a charming local toy store known for its delightful window displays, and it had always held a special place in the hearts of the townspeople. Today, the display featured an array of plush cats, each with a unique pattern and expression, nestled amongst a miniature winter wonderland scene.

Abigail paused, her breath fogging up the glass as she peered through the window. The plush cats looked so inviting, their furry coats and friendly faces seeming to beckon her closer. A thought struck her. How wonderful it would be to gift these plush cats to the children in the hospital ward, to bring them some joy on this festive day. She imagined their faces lighting up at the sight of these cuddly companions. It seemed like the perfect way to extend the spirit of kindness she had rediscovered.

She reached for the door, only to find it locked. A small sign hung there, reading "Closed for Christmas." Disappointment washed over her. She hadn't thought of this in time, and now it was too late to make it happen. The realization that even with her newfound perspective, she couldn't act on every good intention, was sobering.

Sighing softly, she stepped back from the store, her eyes lingering on the plush cats a moment longer. There was a sense of what could have been – a small gesture which might have made a big difference. The snow continued to fall, covering the storefront and the dreams it held within.

Shaking off the feeling of regret, she reminded herself that today was about mending bridges and rebuilding relationships, starting with her nephew, Charlie. She continued on her way, the image of the plush cats lingering in her mind, a symbol of the kindness she wanted to carry forward, even if she had missed this opportunity.

Abigail stood on the doorstep of what should be her nephew's home, and took in a deep breath. She considered knocking, then wrestled her phone out of her pocket to check the time. Was it too early? What if he didn't answer the door? What if he wasn't home? If he wasn't, then she had two hot cocoas. The thought of drinking two consecutive hot cocoas was too much too soon. The door opened, interrupting her thought process. Charlie stood before her, dressed smartly, a look of surprise on his face which rivaled Abigail's own expression. After a beat, his face broke into a wide smile.

"Aunt Abigail!"

"Charlie! Hi."

"Hi."

They stood, in an uncomfortable silence – Abigail on the front step and Charlie in the doorway - until Abigail remembered she was still holding a tray of hot cocoas.

"Merry Christmas!" She held up the tray between them as if it was a peace offering. "I'm sorry. I wasn't sure what to get you, so I thought I would start with some hot cocoa from the café."

"Merry Christmas!" Charlie reached his arm up and out at an awkward angle, his hand a claw descending on one of the take-out cups. "Thank you. You really can't go wrong with hot cocoa." With a few squeaky twists he extracted the hot cocoa from the tray. "Especially when it's from there." Charlie took a sip.

"Oh, that reminds me. Margot said to tell you she wishes you a Merry Christmas, too."

"Ah, that's Margot for you." Charlie said. "Thanks for passing on her message."

"Sorry, I should have called you before stopping by. You look like you're going somewhere." Abigail took her cup out of the tray. She looked around for someplace to put the tray, then shrugged and started to stuff it into her purse. Charlie stifled a laugh – there was no way it was going to fit in her purse – then, held out his hand to take the tray.

"Oh, thanks," Abigail let out a nervous laugh.

"Don't mention it," Charlie frisbeed the tray into his house. "I'm not really going anywhere. Just heading out for a walk to take in the magic of Christmas morning."

Abigail laughed again, she wasn't sure exactly why.

"Would you like to join me?" Charlie asked.

"Sure. I'd love to. Thank you."

Charlie stepped outside, closed the door behind him and locked it. He pocketed his keys and turned to Abigail.

"Let's go."

After a few minutes of silently sipping their hot cocoa, Charlie couldn't keep it to himself any longer.

"I went to your house!" He took a quick swig of cocoa.

"What?" Abigail stopped in her tracks. "This morning?"

"No," Charlie shook his head. "Yesterday morning."

"Oh," Abigail relaxed and started walking again. "You knew I wouldn't be home yesterday morning."

"Yeah," Charlie kept pace with her. "I was just going to leave it in your mailbox."

"What made you change your mind?"

"I don't know. I opened the mailbox lid and was about to drop it inside," Charlie shrugged his shoulders. "Then I was overcome with a sensation of terror. . . 'What if she doesn't check her mailbox? She'll think I didn't get her a card!'" The cocoa cup almost slipped from his hand as he pantomimed his reaction.

"Oh, you-" Abigail couldn't help but smile at his antics and gave him a gentle nudge with her elbow. "Wait a minute. So that means those were your footprints on my doorstep!"

"Guilty."

"I'm glad you changed your mind. You were probably right. I would never have found it. Your card is the only one I received this year."

Charlie stared at his aunt in astonishment. "No."

"Mm-hmm," Abigail turned to her nephew with eyes that said 'Would I lie to you?' so clearly he could almost hear them.

"No!" Charlie was appalled. "I can't believe it. You mean to tell me everyone in Little Dickens was okay with coming to ask for donations, but couldn't be bothered to give you a Christmas card?!"

"I know, right?" Abigail looked at him again. *How did I never see that there was someone on my side?* "The nerve!" She began to laugh and Charlie joined in. After their laughter finally subsided, she held her stomach and smiled. "I needed that."

"Me, too." Charlie said, then his face clouded over.

"What is it?"

"Not even Susan?" Charlie asked.

Abigail took a deep breath before answering.

"I think she's had a lot on her mind... Speaking of Susan ... "

"Yesss?"

"She's my next stop. I need to tell her something, and it has to be done in person."

"On Christmas morning?"

"Yes."

"Is it business?" Charlie gave her the same side-eye look as Margot did earlier at the cafe.

"Well, yeesss. But it's not what you're thinking. It's just – well – why don't you come along with me?"

"Are you using me as a buffer?"

"No, now let's get back to my car."

"Lead the way. To the Carson-mobile!"

Now it was Abigail's turn to give her nephew the side-eye.

Chapter Ten

Abigail rang the doorbell. Charlie gave her a nervous smile while they waited on Susan's doorstep.

"She hung up the wreath," he pointed at the wreath hanging on the door.

"She did."

"I've never been here before."

"You haven't? Neither have I. I know my excuse. What's yours?"

Charlie looked down at the ground and discovered that pushing aside some snow with his right foot required all his attention. Until the door opened up.

Susan was wearing one of her ugly Christmas sweaters and blue jeans. On her feet were green elf slippers.

"Abigail! And Charlie. . . is this a social call?"

"Yes. Yes it is. I'm . . . we're here to wish you a Merry Christmas." Abigail gestured to include Charlie.

"Merry Christmas." Charlie gave Susan an awkward wave. This made it three days in a row he'd seen her and he was now questioning the wisdom of so quickly accepting his aunt's invitation to join her for this visit.

"May we come in?" Abigail asked.

Susan took a moment to think about this. Then she opened the door wider and stepped back to let them in.

"Sure."

Susan led Abigail and Charlie down the long hallway.

"Tim?" she called out. "We have some visitors."

Charlie looked at Abigail, confused. She grabbed his hand and gave it a light squeeze.

"Just wait," she whispered.

The first thing the visitors saw when they entered the living room was the light from the Christmas tree. Appearing to be basking in its glow was Tim, seated in his wheelchair. Curled up on his lap was a Siamese cat. He looked up from petting the cat when they entered the room.

"Tim. This is Abigail and Charlie Carson. Abigail, Charlie, this is Tim, my brother."

"Merry Christmas! Susan has told me a lot about both of you." He wheeled his chair closer and shook their hands. Then he looked over at his sister. "And she never mentioned me because I asked her not to."

"Why?" asked Charlie, puzzled.

Abigail and Susan shared a quick glance before Tim answered Charlie's question.

"I didn't want to be seen. I didn't want people looking at me and feeling sorry for me. I was afraid I'd feel even more sorry for myself if I was around other people."

"At least you had your sister," Charlie looked from Tim to Susan.

"Yeah. I don't know what I would've done without Susan," Tim scratched his head. "I haven't always been the easiest person to be around the last year or so."

"Year or so. Who are you kidding?" Susan let out a scoff. "You've always had moments where you're insufferable."

Tim shrugged and grinned shamelessly at her remark.

Abigail couldn't stand it any longer. She had to ask.

"And where did you get that cat?"

"The strangest thing. It was sleeping under the tree when we got up this morning," Tim wheeled around a bit to point to the location under the tree where they found the Siamese. The unmistakable whiff of love and togetherness hung around the cat like an ethereal aura.

Susan shrugged her shoulders. "I have no idea where it came from or how it got in here."

"Well, it seems to have made itself right at home." Abigail made her way over to Tim and the Siamese. The air was filled with the perfume of hope and joy. She held her breath and pet the cat. Nothing happened. "Hmm."

Hearing her slightly perplexed hum, Tim looked at her and asked, "Did you think something was going to happen?"

"It is Christmas after all. You never know!" Abigail replied as she went back to Charlie's side. "Susan, uh, I came here today because I had some things to tell you that couldn't wait."

Tim and Susan exchanged glances before Tim suggested, "Wait. Should she be sitting down?"

This prompted laughter from Abigail. "Maybe."

"You just laughed." Susan pointed at the nearest chair. "I'm sitting down."

"That's fair." Abigail laughed again before continuing. "I haven't been the most fun person to be around lately. And I own up to that. And that's going to change. Effective immediately. Also effective immediately, Susan, you are officially a partner in Carson Developments. Provided you accept, of course."

"I do!"

"I'm pretty sure it was a partnership not a marriage proposal," Tim said.

Susan grabbed the nearest throw pillow and threw it at Tim.

"I accept! I can hardly believe it. Abigail, is this actually happening?"

"Yes, it is." Abigail looked at Tim and the cat. "And there is one more thing that is effective immediately. We are closing down the business for two months."

The announcement caused Charlie and Tim to gape in surprise along with Susan who uttered her confusion aloud:

"What? Why?"

Abigail looked at them all. "The project is stalled while we're waiting for approvals. I know there are other things we can do in the meantime. But I think we've both been pushing so hard on this project, it is time for this break. I know I need it. I've needed it for longer than I care to admit. If not now, when?"

"If not now, when?" Susan repeated, feeling like she must be in a dream.

"That sounds like a cat poster," Tim said.

Charlie laughed and pointed at the cat on Tim's lap. "It really does." Abigail shook her head and looked over at Susan.

"So, how about it? As an official partner, do you agree to a two month break?"

"Do I ever!" Susan stood up and walked over to Abigail. They shook hands and then shared a brief hug.

"So what are you going to do with two months off?" Tim asked.

Abigail went over to Charlie and put her hand on his shoulder. "For one thing, I'm going to spend some time getting to know my family."

"That sounds wonderful, Aunt Abigail," A huge grin broke out over Charlie's face.

"And what about you, Susan?" Abigail asked.

"Well . . . the first thing that comes to mind is Tim's surgery. We can see if there's an opening. There's a lot to do before and after."

"Will two months be enough?'

"We won't know until it happens," Tim said. "It could take that long for something to open up."

"What about another hospital?" Abigail asked. "I know we all want to support local, but maybe local isn't the best place for this surgery."

"That's a good suggestion. They've actually recommended another surgeon from outside this area as one of the best. But, we never could make the time for the trip."

"If it's not an imposition, I'd love to help out however I can. Driving, making arrangements for accommodations, you need it, you name it," said Abigail.

Charlie added, "I won't have two months off, but I'd love to help out, too."

"Thank you, both," said Susan. "I'll let you know once we figure out steps we need to take in the new year.'

"Wow, I really appreciate this," Tim said. "This is probably the best Christmas present I've got since I was a kid."

"Better than the football?" Susan asked.

"Way better than the football."

"I'd better get Charlie back home," said Abigail. "It was wonderful to meet you, Tim. Merry Christmas."

"Merry Christmas," Tim waved goodbye to Abigail and Charlie.

Abigail and Susan headed to the front door.

Charlie walked over to Tim to shake his hand again in farewell.

"It was great to meet you, Tim. Merry Christmas."

Tim kept Charlie's hand in his grip, he craned his head to check that Susan was out of earshot.

"Thank you for the wreath. It really made Susan happy." He let go of Charlie's hand.

"Really?" Charlie asked, no longer annoyed with Tim for nearly crushing his hand in a vicelike grip for longer than necessary. "I appreciate you telling me. I . . . I hoped she would like it."

Tim checked again that Susan was still out of earshot. Even then he lowered his voice as he said, "It's not just the wreath she likes."

"You mean-?" Charlie was taken aback that Susan's brother, of all people, was hinting that she liked him. He'd expected the typical over-protective big brother routine.

"Why don't you ask her?"

"Wait. You are the older sibling aren't you?"

Tim nodded and lobbed the pillow Susan had thrown at him right into Charlie's face.

Meanwhile, at the door, Susan and Abigail continued their own discussion.

"Abigail? What happened? You were acting a bit unlike yourself recently. Are you-Are you well?"

Abigail laughed in response.

"And laughing again. I'm tempted to think that we're in the Twilight Zone and you've been switched with a pod person or something."

Abigail laughed again before she pulled herself together to respond. "It really must seem like I have been. Switched! I mean – I've been focusing on all the wrong things for all the right reasons. Sometimes life is sending you the signals but you just can't see them. That was me, until a few days ago. When life decided to send me some signals that I couldn't ignore."

"Okay, signals. From life itself. Details," said Susan.

"That's all I'm ready to say for now." Abigail raised her hands to shoulder level. "It's been a surreal experience."

Charlie burst into the doorway and reeled back to stop himself from crashing into them.

"Sorry, I got chatting with Tim," he said. "Are you ready?"

Abigail nodded, opened the door and stepped outside, waving goodbye to Susan.

"Oh, before I forget. Susan, here's my card." Charlie dug into the inside pocket of his jacket and extracted the business card. "For a coding company, it sure is old-fashioned. I didn't think people used these things anymore."

"Yet you're carrying them around with you?" Susan took the card from him.

"Yeah, I forget I have them and by the time I remember, it's usually too late." Charlie scratched the back of his head, absent-mindedly. "I hope it's not too late."

Susan thought about this for a moment, then asked "Is it ever too late when it's Christmas?"

"Good point." Charlie couldn't keep the smile from spreading over his face.

"I'll call you later."

"Great." Charlie stepped outside to join his aunt.

Abigail and Charlie began their descent of the stairs.

"Do you have any more of those cards, Charlie?"

Charlie reached inside his jacket, dug around a bit and pulled a card out.

"May I have that one?"

"Sure!" Charlie handed the card over to Abigail.

"Now I can phone you instead of turning up unexpectedly on your doorstep."

They had reached the bottom of the stairs and were on their way to the sidewalk when Abigail pulled her phone out to add Charlie's number. The phone's screen displayed a missed call notification. The caller ID showed the call was from a Dr. Ifhram, the one she delivered the check to.

"That's odd. Why would they be calling me? There can't be a problem with the check I gave them."

Abigail pressed the call button to dial.

After a couple of rings Dr. Ifhram answered. "Merry Christmas. Dr. Ifhram speaking."

"Hello, Dr. Ifhram. This is Abigail Carson. I'm sorry I missed your call-"

"Ms. Carson! You should have told us what you had planned."

"I'm sorry?"

"Hold on. I'll switch to video call." The phone hung up and when Abigail answered, the video switched on. On the screen Abigail and Charlie could see behind the doctor. She was standing in the middle of the Children's ward. Each child had a plush cat they were playing with.

"Don't be sorry." The doctor panned their phone around the room, to show the children were laughing and playing. Some were smiling with pure joy while hugging their plush toys. "Just let us know next time, please. I just have to know . . . How did you know all the kids' names?"

Abigail glanced down the street and spotted Jacob standing in front of the town's small church.

"A little elf told me."

Dr. Ifhram and the children in the ward chorused. "Merry Christmas!"

Abigail waved and said "Merry Christmas!"

She ended the call and put the phone away.

Charlie couldn't hide his amazement at what he'd just witnessed. "What was that all about?"

"Just some Christmas Spirit spreading good cheer. I'll fill you in later," Abigail shook her head, even though she knew it wouldn't clear up the confusion. She pointed over to the church. "Would you give me a few minutes, please, Charlie?"

"Sure."

Abigail walked over to where Jacob was standing. He turned from the road to look at the church. Abigail appreciated the maneuver. With their backs to Charlie, he wouldn't see what would look like Abigail talking to herself.

"You shouldn't have done that." The words were out of her mouth before she could stop herself.

"Why not?" Jacob leaned back as if dodging a blow. "You would've done it if you had thought of it in time."

"True, but I didn't think of it in time."

"Consider it a going away Christmas present, then."

Abigail nodded. She could accept that.

"So what happens now? The Christmas bells ring and you get your wings?"

Jacob let out a chuckle before he replied. "I think you've got your Christmas specials mixed up. That's not what happens. Besides, we both know I'm no angel."

"Oh, I don't know about that." Abigail looked at him out of the corner of her eye. "You came back to help me."

"No, don't give me credit for that." Jacob said. "I was sent back."

"No one made you give those toys to the Children's ward."

Jacob threw his hands up in the air and looked down at the ground.

"You can argue my case all you want. It doesn't matter. It's too late for me. It's the deeds we do while we are living that matter." He turned his head to look at Abigail. "I sealed my fate long ago."

Jacob waited for Abigail to say something. He saw her inhale sharply, her eyes widen. He followed her gaze and saw all three Cats of Christmas were sitting before them.

The Cat of Christmas Present meowed. *Normally that is true. But we are Christmas Spirits and we have extra powers available to us this time of year.*

"What are you saying?" Jacob asked.

Abigail turned her head and looked at Jacob. "Can you understand them?"

Jacob nodded.

Abigail looked back to the cats in front of them. "All I hear is 'Meow.'"

The Cat of Christmas Past meowed. *We haven't only been watching Abigail. We've been watching you, too.*

"Meow," said the Cat of Christmas Present. *In life, you didn't get the intervention Abigail did. We didn't think it would be enough, we were too late. But, this was your second chance, Jacob.*

"What are they saying?" Abigail leaned over and whispered to Jacob.

"They said that it was too late for me to change in life. This was my second chance." He said to Abigail, then asked the Cats, "Why didn't you tell me?

"Meow," said the Cat of Christmas Past. *You had to do it for Abigail, not yourself.*

The Cat of Christmas Present meowed. *And you did. You even stayed longer than you should have to help us guide her.*

"Well?" Abigail felt left out of the loop.

Jacob translated, "They say they couldn't have done it without me."

The Cat of Christmas Future growled. Both Jacob and Abigail jumped, surprised to hear the large cat make a sound.

"Okay," Jacob extended an arm out to the Cat of Christmas Future. "Okay, they didn't say that exactly. But they say I helped."

"Yes, you did," Abigail swung her arms and shuffled her feet nervously. "It was good to get the chance to see you again. I thought I never would."

Jacob raised an eyebrow at Abigail and grinned.

"What's so amusing about that?"

"The nervous footwork. It's a Carson family trait. More pronounced in the males." Jacob tilted his head back to indicate Charlie.

A soft smile appeared on Abigail's face. "I'd forgotten."

"Meow," said the Cat of Christmas Present. *It's time to go.*

"They say it's time to go," said Jacob

"Then it's time to go. You can't argue with the cats of Christmas," said Abigail.

The Cats of Christmas Past and Present sprang up and let out happy meows.

"Merry Christmas, Abigail."

"Merry Christmas, Jacob."

Charlie worked up the courage to go over to his aunt as Jacob and the Cats of Christmas faded away.

"Is everything okay?"

Abigail turned to Charlie and straightened out his scarf before she answered.

"Yes, for the first time in a long time, everything is okay."

Author Acknowledgements

I'd like to start off by apologizing to anyone who I miss including in these acknowledgements. There are so many people who have supported me in this journey.

First, the great author himself, Charles Dickens, for writing and self-publishing the book that inspired this and countless other retellings.

Scribe Meets World for helping to plant the idea that this could maybe be a thing.

Sandra Wickham and her Feel Write Again Writers Group, for helping to get the idea out of my head and into an outline and first draft.

My inherited friend, Jean, who isn't that keen on cats but supports her writer friend. Jean, your support and not-so-gentle prodding is one of the reasons this book is finished.

My semiannual breakfast (and sometimes supper) group, you know who you are. I may have missed some deadlines (what writer doesn't) but your encouragement and interest helped me to finish the book.

The wonderful cover design team at GetCovers.com. Your patience and assistance in revising the cover from a stand alone to Book 1 of a series is appreciated. It was arranged and completed so quickly, an absolute pleasure to work with.

Author's Notes

There is a lifetime of reading and watching adaptations of "A Christmas Carol" in Meowy Christmas. Christmas is that special time of year when you get to watch old favorites over and over again. And listen to your favorite Christmas carols and songs. When the idea for this retelling came to me, I wasn't sure how I was going to pull it off. Then I found out about animal-assisted therapy and I found my answer. Animal-assisted therapy (AAT) has become increasingly recognized and has been incorporated into a range of medical settings across North America. The animals used in AAT are specially trained to ensure they are well-behaved and safe to interact with patients. I took some artistic license with the Cat of Christmas Present, but interaction with animals can provide comfort, encourage social interactions and help reduce stress.

If you'd like to delve into more detail about animal-assisted therapy, here are links to two sources:

National Library of Medicine. Animal assisted intervention: A systematic review of benefits and risks (2016):

https://www.ncbi.nlm.nih.gov/pmc/articles/PMC7185850/

MedicalNewsToday. What to know about animal therapy (2020:

https://www.medicalnewstoday.com/articles/animal-therapy

The first two drafts of Meowy Christmas were as a stand alone novel. Going over the second draft, I realized how much the town of Little Dickens had grown and the potential it held. It seemed a shame to only visit Little Dickens once. So I looked at the cast of characters and the situations that would allow me to return to it. By the third draft, Meowy Christmas had become Book 1 in the Christmas in Little Dickens series. I hope that you are looking forward to returning to Little Dickens, Oregon as much as I am. I've already made a start on Book 2, Frosty Footprints. The work in progress Chapter 1 follows. I must put in this disclaimer: the artwork and the chapter that follow are early drafts, when Book 2 is finished and published, the final version may be different from what is included here with Book 1.

About the Author

Carol Appleyard, a name synonymous with the enchantment of Christmas, has a heart that beats in tune with the festive season's timeless melodies. An avid enthusiast of Christmas music and movies, she believes these joyous tunes and tales are not just for December, but for cherishing all year round. However, she firmly upholds the tradition of waiting until December 1st to deck the halls and light up the festive decor.

Amidst her Yuletide spirit, Carol harbors a deep fondness for felines. Her love for cats is as profound as her affection for Christmas, creating a perfect blend of interests that inspired her debut in the world of fiction. "Meowy Christmas," her maiden literary venture, is more than just a book; it's a reflection of her love for these two passions intertwined.

While Carol is currently without a cat companion, this has only given her more time to dream up her festive stories. Her first book, "Meowy Christmas," is a charming reflection of her love for the holiday season and its furry friends.

As Carol Appleyard continues to explore her storytelling, readers can look forward to more tales that capture the warmth and joy of Christmas, and the endearing antics of cats. "Meowy Christmas" is just the beginning of her journey in celebrating these delightful themes.

CAROL APPLEYARD

BOOK 2

Frosty Footprints

M eet Susan Cardinal, an indigenous architect who is settling into her new role as partner at Cardinal and Carson Developments. Alongside her business partner, Abigail Carson, and their new assistant, Ethan Clarke, Susan eagerly anticipates the grand opening of the Little Dickens Community Center.

Balancing the demands of her career, the recovery of her brother Tim from surgery, and a rekindling romance with the charming Charlie Carson, Susan embraces the budding excitement that Christmas brings to the town.

Amidst the twinkling lights and the joyous holiday preparations, Little Dickens prepares for an Indigenous storytelling event that promises to capture the essence of their diverse community. Susan finds herself on a journey of love, friendship, community spirit, and personal discovery, all leading up to a Christmas celebration that may forever change her life.

Join Susan Cardinal as she navigates the uncertainties of her personal and professional life, weaving together a tapestry of warmth, growth, and new beginnings. Delve into "Frosty Footprints," the heartwarming second installment in the Christmas in Little Dickens series, and immerse yourself in a world where love, community, and the magic of the holiday season intertwine.

CAROL APPLEYARD

BOOK 2

Frosty Footprints

Chapter 1

A frosty morning enveloped Little Dickens, Oregon like a sparkling white blanket, the air crisp and invigorating. Christmas was fast approaching, and the town had already begun to sprout festive decorations – twinkling lights strung from lampposts, wreaths hung on doors, and storefront windows painted with snowy scenes.

Susan Cardinal stepped off the bus, her breath forming small clouds as she exhaled. She pulled her scarf tighter around her neck, her brown eyes taking in the familiar sights of Little Dickens. It was a postcard come to life. Being away on a work trip for just a few days had made her realize how much she had come to love this place since moving here, though she still felt like a visitor.

"Welcome back, Susan!" called out Margot, the owner of the Cocoa Café, as she swept snow from her doorstep. "How was your trip?"

"Thanks, Margot," Susan replied with a smile. "It went well. We secured a new contract for a housing development."

"That's great news! It's refreshing to see someone bringing innovative ideas to our town," Margot commented. Susan felt a pang of guilt, realizing she had shared the news with Margot before she's had the chance to mention it to Ethan Clarke, the new assistant at Cardinal & Carson and a close friend of both Margot and herself.

She had just returned from a work trip to the city, and was glad to be back. Little Dickens was beginning to feel like home, more than any other place she had lived. As she walked briskly down the snowy sidewalk, Susan made a silent promise to immerse herself more in the community and its traditions this Christmas season.

The snow-covered ground sparkled under the early morning sun, and the scent of pine needles filled the air. Susan smiled, feeling a sense of belonging wash over her.

In her partnership at the property development company Cardinal and Carson, she had forged a strong bond with her business partner, Abigail Carson. Despite the playful rivalry over the company's name, Susan cherished the opportunity Abigail had given her to grow and contribute to their shared vision.

As Susan walked towards their office building, she saw Abigail's car in the parking lot. She knew that her business partner had just returned from a brief work trip, and as she got closer to the entrance, she could see Abigail waiting for her at the door.

"Good morning, Susan," Abigail greeted her with a warm smile.

"Good morning, Abigail," Susan replied, returning the smile. "How was your trip?"

"Busy, as always," Abigail said, shaking her head. "But it's good to be back home."

"Home" - Susan repeated the word silently to herself, feeling a sense of pride and contentment fill her heart. This small town had become her home too, ever since she moved here to work with Abigail. They had both worked long and hard after the unexpected death of the founder of the company, Jacob Morris. But now, they stood at the threshold of their triumph - the grand opening of the Little Dickens Community Center, a project developed by Cardinal and Carson Developments.

Their dedication and tireless efforts had paid off, and now, they could feel the anticipation building in the air. It was a few days before the grand opening, and Ethan Clarke, the newest member of their team, had been diligently working to prepare the space for the upcoming event.

After wrapping up their morning tasks at the office, Susan joined Abigail in her car for the short drive to the community center. Susan settled into the passenger seat. As Abigail navigated through the familiar streets of their small town, the conversation flowed effortlessly between them.

"So, how are things shaping up for the grand opening?" Susan asked, adjusting the sun visor to block the glare of the morning sun.

Abigail glanced at her with a mixture of pride and relief. "Everything's on track, thanks to Ethan's hard work. He's really stepped up, you know."

Susan nodded, her thoughts briefly on their newest team member. "He's been a great addition to the team. I'm glad we brought him on board."

"How's Tim doing?" Abigail asked as she navigated through a quiet street. She had always shown a genuine interest in Susan's family, especially since Tim's surgery six months ago.

Susan's face brightened at the mention of her brother. "He's doing surprisingly well. His recovery has been smoother than we expected. The doctors are really pleased with his progress."

"That's great to hear," Abigail responded. "He's been through so much."

"Yeah, it's been a tough journey, but he's incredibly resilient. Just last week, he started walking with a cane. It's a big milestone for him," Susan shared, her pride in her brother's courage clear.

Abigail glanced over with admiration. "That's remarkable. He must be so relieved to be regaining his independence."

Susan nodded, her thoughts briefly with Tim. "He is. And he's already talking about finding his own place to live, though I've told him there's no rush."

The car slowed as they approached a traffic light. "He's lucky to have your support," Abigail said, turning to look at Susan. "Having family around during recovery makes all the difference."

Susan sighed softly, grateful for the bond she shared with her brother. "It does. And I'm just thankful things are looking up for him."

"That's good to hear," Abigail said, her tone optimistic yet cautious. "After all the hurdles we've faced, it feels like we're finally moving forward."

Susan sensed the unspoken reference to their past challenges. "We've come a long way, haven't we? From fighting off takeovers to now opening our own community center."

Abigail smiled, her eyes reflecting in the rearview mirror. "It's been quite a journey. But I wouldn't change a thing. It's all been worth it."

Not long after the light turned green they were pulling into the community center's parking lot. Susan felt a sense of contentment. Her professional achievements with Abigail, alongside her brother Tim's recovery, filled her with a profound sense of gratitude.

As they entered the main hall, their eyes widened with awe. The space was transformed into a vibrant hub of activity, a stark contrast to its previous state of emptiness. People bustled around, setting up displays, hanging decorations, and adjusting the lighting to create the perfect ambiance.

"Wow," Susan whispered, her voice filled with admiration as she scanned the room.

Abigail nodded in agreement, a look of pride in her eyes. "Ethan has done an incredible job, hasn't he? This place is going to be a true gem for the community. It really is the gift that keeps on giving." Susan couldn't agree more. She knew that this community center was more than just a business venture; it was a symbol of their dedication to this town and its people.

As they continued to explore the space, they couldn't help but overhear a conversation between some of the event organizers nearby.

"Did you hear about the seating arrangements?" one of them said with a chuckle. "It seems Ethan made sure our names were on the reserved seats list."

Susan grinned at the mention of Ethan's thoughtful gesture.

Abigail chuckled. "Well, Ethan's certainly made his mark, hasn't he?"

It was a colorful flyer on the community center's bulletin board that caught Susan's eye. It advertised an upcoming Indigenous story-telling event, focusing on winter tales and legends, including those about Sasquatch. The flyer was beautifully designed, evoking a sense of mystery and wonder.

"Look at this, Abigail," Susan said, pointing to the flyer. "Have you heard about this storytelling event?"

Abigail leaned in to read. "Oh, the Indigenous storytelling night? Yes, I've heard. It's supposed to be quite an experience, with winter tales and Sasquatch legends."

A shiver of excitement ran down Susan's spine. She had always been in-trigued by the local Sasquatch stories. "I'm definitely going," she declared. "It sounds fascinating. Are you interested?"

Abigail smiled but shook her head. "I have other plans that day, but you should definitely go. It sounds right up your alley."

Throughout the day, Susan's thoughts kept drifting back to the flyer. The stories promised an adventure, a dive into the unknown that might illuminate her own path of self-discovery. She felt a thrilling mix of excite-ment and anticipation at the prospect of attending the event.

The warm, inviting scent of freshly brewed coffee and chocolate wafted through the crisp winter air as Susan approached Margot's Cocoa Café. The café was a popular spot among Little Dickens' locals, with twinkling fairy lights that illuminated the frost-covered windows. She stepped inside, grateful for the reprieve from the cold, and scanned the cozy establishment for an empty table. She spotted one near the window, but as she made her way over, she collided with someone.

"Sorry," she said, looking up to see Charlie Carson.

"Hey, no problem," Charlie replied.

They stood there for a moment, awkwardly trying to find something to say. Susan couldn't help but notice how handsome Charlie looked in his plaid shirt and jeans.

"Who knew how awkward it would be to go on a date with your business partner's nephew?' Charlie broke the silence. "Maybe we could, you know, give it another shot?"

Before Susan could respond, Margot, the owner of the café, appeared beside them with a warm smile. "Why don't you two take a seat by the window? I'll bring over your favorites," she said, gesturing towards the table Susan had spotted earlier.

Surprised yet relieved, Susan and Charlie followed Margot's suggestion. True to her word, Margot soon arrived with two steaming mugs of hot chocolate, topped with a swirl of whipped cream and a sprinkle of cocoa powder. "Here you go, on the house. I thought you might need these," she said with a wink, before returning to the counter.

Holding the warm mugs, they shared a smile, both grateful for Margot's timely rescue from their awkward standstill.

"Really?" Susan finally responded to Charlie's earlier proposition, her cheeks flushed but her eyes hopeful.

"Really," Charlie confirmed, his gaze steady on hers over the rim of his mug.

Susan felt a warmth spread through her body at Charlie's words. She had been so busy with work and exploring her heritage that she hadn't thought much about romance lately.

"Okay," she said, smiling at him. "Let's do it."

Susan and Charlie sat across from each other, their hands wrapped around steaming mugs.

Susan took a sip of her hot chocolate, relishing the rich, creamy taste. "So, what have you been up to lately, Charlie?"

Charlie leaned back in his chair, looking thoughtful. "Well, I've been working on this new tech project. It's been keeping me pretty busy."

He took a sip of his hot chocolate, gathering his thoughts. "So...tell me what you've been up to. Any cool new projects?"

Susan nodded, her eyes lighting up. "I've been working on some designs that incorporate Indigenous influences. Subtle things that highlight the connection between people and nature."

"That sounds amazing," he said. He realized there was so much more to her than he had known, layers of depth and dedication that he found compelling. "It's so cool how you're exploring your heritage through your work."

"Speaking of–" Susan said, her gaze lingering on the twinkling lights for a moment before returning to Charlie, "there's actually an event coming up that you might find interesting." She hesitated for a moment, unsure how he would react to her suggestion. "It's an Indigenous storytelling gathering here in Little Dickens. They focus on winter tales and legends, including some about Sasquatch."

Charlie raised his eyebrows, intrigued. "Really? That sounds fascinating."

"Would you... would you like to come with me?" Susan asked, half-expecting him to decline. She fiddled with the handle of her mug, her heart racing as she awaited his response.

"Absolutely, I'd love to," Charlie replied without hesitation. His interest was piqued not only by the cultural aspect but also by the opportunity to know Susan on a deeper level. "When is it?"

"Next Saturday evening," she answered, relief and excitement evident in her eyes. "I'll make sure to send you all the details."

"Sounds great," Charlie said with a smile, "I've always been interested in stories and cultures. And learning about this part of your life, it's... it's really fascinating."

Susan wasn't just another person he met in Little Dickens; she was someone who had carved a unique path for herself. And that was something he found irresistibly intriguing.

"Great," Susan said, her cheeks flushing with a mix of pleasure and embarrassment over her earlier assumption. "I'll text you the details later."

As they prepared to leave Margot's Cocoa Café, Tim Cardinal showed up at the doorway, leaning casually on his cane. His face lit up with a playful grin as he took in the sight in front of him.

"Hey sis," he greeted Susan, nodding at Charlie. "You two finally going on another date?"

"Tim!" Susan scolded, laughter dancing in her eyes. "It's not like that. We're just attending the Indigenous storytelling event together."

"Ah, winter tales and what-not, huh?" Tim raised an eyebrow, turning to Charlie. "Better you than me."

"Come on, Tim," Susan chided, playfully swatting her brother's arm. "It'll be interesting, I promise."

"Alright, alright," Tim conceded, grinning at the good-natured banter. "Just don't say I didn't warn you." He looked at Charlie, trying to gauge his reaction. "But seriously, enjoy the event. You might find it more enlightening than you expect."

"Thanks, Tim," Charlie responded, his voice warm and sincere. "I appreciate the encouragement."

Susan and Tim began their journey home, their footsteps crunching on the freshly fallen snow. She couldn't contain her excitement, stealing glances back at Charlie who waved goodbye with a warm smile. The thought of the upcoming Indigenous storytelling event, which they had planned to attend together, filled her with an indescribable sense of anticipation.

They passed by a flyer for the event, pinned against the rough bark of an old tree. It reminded Susan of the ancient tales that would soon be shared, of elders weaving stories that bridged generations, and of children, eyes wide with wonder, absorbing the wisdom of their ancestors. This imagery filled her with a deep sense of pride and belonging.

Tim, walking beside her, seemed lost in thought, his brow furrowed in contemplation. Susan knew he struggled with doubts about fully embracing their heritage. After all, they had been raised largely disconnected from it. Squeezing his arm reassuringly, she offered gentle words, "I know it's unfamiliar, but I believe we'll find our place here in time."

Taking a deep breath of the crisp winter air, Susan's thoughts drifted back to Charlie. A hint of a smile played at her lips as she recalled their encounter at the cafe. Underneath that slightly awkward and bumbling exterior, she sensed a kind-hearted soul who was genuinely interested in learning about her culture.

The town of Little Dickens was a spectacle of holiday joy. Elaborate decorations adorned the streets, and twinkling lights wrapped around lampposts and storefronts. The cold air nipped playfully at their noses and cheeks, enhancing the enchantment of the season. "Absolutely stunning," Susan remarked, her voice a whisper of awe.

Tim nodded, his gaze sweeping across the vibrant community. Despite being newcomers, the bond within this close-knit town was palpable, exuding a warmth and familiarity that was comforting.

As they continued their walk through the quaint streets of Little Dickens, Susan couldn't help but feel a strong connection to this place. Though they hadn't grown up here, there was something about the people and traditions that made her feel like she belonged.

The town seemed to come alive with holiday cheer - colorful wreaths and red ribbons adorned storefronts while cheerful music filled the air. The smell of fresh pine and warm cinnamon wafted around them as they passed by the outdoor Christmas market. Locals bundled up in scarves and mittens sold handmade crafts and treats, adding to the festive charm of the town.

Susan's attention was caught by the shimmering lights that decorated the town. The faint scent of pine and cinnamon filled the air, transporting her to a realm of childhood memories and holiday magic. Tim's cane tapped rhythmically against the cobblestone streets, providing a steady beat to the bustling preparations around them.

"Wow, look at that!" Susan exclaimed, pointing to a group of children building an elaborate snow fort in the town square. Their laughter rang out like silver bells, their rosy cheeks and frost-kissed noses highlighting their joy for all to see. "I remember doing that when we were kids."

"Me too," Tim said, grinning as he watched the youngsters hard at work. "You always insisted on being the general, commanding us all from your icy throne."

Susan chuckled, recalling her bossy younger self with fondness. "Well, someone had to keep you all in line."

"True enough," Tim said, his smile widening.

As they moved along, Susan took note of the townspeople gathered together in clusters, sharing festive treats and stories, their faces alight with excitement and anticipation. As if on cue, a group of carolers emerged from a nearby church, their harmonious voices filling the crisp air with beloved melodies. It was a scene straight out of a Christmas card.

"Maybe I could volunteer for one of the holiday events this year," Susan said, mulling over the possibilities. "Like the tree lighting ceremony, or helping with the food drive."

"Sounds like a great idea, sis," Tim said.

"Plus," she added, a playful glint in her eye, "And who knows? Maybe I'll even rope Charlie into helping."

Tim laughed, clearly amused by the idea. "I'm sure he wouldn't mind. After all, he did agree to come to the storytelling event with you."

"True," Susan mused, a warmth spreading through her chest as she thought of the budding connection between herself and Charlie.

"Hey Tim, you know," Susan said, pausing to look at the wreath, "this wreath reminds me of the one Charlie gave me last Christmas, before our first date." The sight of it sparked a bittersweet memory, a reminder of the time when their feelings for each other were present but still unspoken, a silent acknowledgment of the potential that was only beginning to unfold between them.

Tim glanced at the wreath, then back at Susan, an understanding smile on his face. "Charlie really played the long game, huh? Crushing on you for almost a year and then starting with that wreath," he said, a blend of admiration and brotherly teasing in his voice. "It's kind of sweet when you think about it."

"Hey, do you remember that time we tried to build a snowman when we were kids?" Susan asked playfully as they passed by an unfinished snowman in someone's yard, its twig arms sticking out at odd angles.

"Of course I do," Tim replied, his eyes twinkling knowingly at her deflection. "I think my hands nearly froze off because we forgot our gloves."

"Sounds like us," Susan chuckled, her breath forming clouds of mist in the frosty air. The memory brought them closer together and reminded her that despite the differences in their perspective towards their heritage, they would always have each other's backs.

As they approached their cozy home, decorated with twinkling lights and some lawn inflatables, Susan couldn't help but feel a sense of belonging. She knew that Little Dickens was a special place, and she was grateful to be a part of it.

"Alright, I'm going to head inside and warm up," Tim said, rubbing his hands together for emphasis. "And remember, don't let Charlie trip over any Sasquatch tracks!"

"Very funny," Susan retorted, rolling her eyes but unable to suppress a grin. As her brother disappeared into the house, she paused on the doorstep, taking a deep breath of the crisp winter air, feeling grateful for this moment, for Little Dickens, and for the new chapter unfolding in her life.

BATWINGED
BOOKS

www.batwingedbooks.com

Follow us on Facebook:
https://www.facebook.com/batwingedbooks

CAROL APPLEYARD

MEOWY CHRISTMAS

BOOK 1

BATWINGED
BOOKS

Book Cover by GetCovers.com

ISBN 978-0-9732533-4-4 (paperback)

ISBN 978-0-9732533-3-7 (ebook)

CAROL APPLEYARD

MEOWY CHRISTMAS

BOOK 1

Christmas
IN
Little Dickens

www.ingramcontent.com/pod-product-compliance
Lightning Source LLC
Chambersburg PA
CBHW052016240626
47153CB00006B/1832